MEGA
MONSTER

David Walliams

MEGA MONSTER

Illustrated by Tony Ross

HarperCollins *Children's Books*

First published in the United Kingdom by
HarperCollins *Children's Books* in 2021
Published in this edition in 2023
HarperCollins *Children's Books* is a division of HarperCollins*Publishers* Ltd,
1 London Bridge Street
London SE1 9GF

www.harpercollins.co.uk

HarperCollins*Publishers*
Macken House, 39/40 Mayor Street Upper
Dublin 1, D01 C9W8, Ireland

1

ISBN 978-0-00-849976-1

For my darling Alfred.
Thank you for giving this book its title.
I love you endlessly.
Daddy x

⌐ PROLOGUE ⌐

Deep in the mists of time, far away from the world we know, is an ancient stone castle. The castle is perched precariously on top of a huge black rock jutting out of a raging sea. The rock is a volcanic island. No one knows for sure when the volcano last erupted or when it might again.

The castle is home to a school. Not just any school. A school where the naughtiest children in the world are sent. It is called **THE CRUEL SCHOOL.**

There is zero chance of escape. The island is many miles away from the mainland, and the sea surrounding it is infested with sharks – hungry sharks who like to gobble up naughty children in one gulp.

There are all sorts of horrors at **THE CRUEL SCHOOL.** The teachers are terrifying, the school dinners are revolting and the lessons will give you nightmares.

So read on, **but only if you dare.**

MEET THE CHARACTERS
IN THIS TALE...
⌐ THE KIDS ⌐

LARKER

The hero of our story earned her nickname by always larking about. She just can't help herself! Larker loves silly jokes, and nothing brings her more joy than making everybody laugh.

SPOD

The great big boy at **THE CRUEL SCHOOL** with missing teeth, a broken nose and a cauliflower ear looks terrifying, but he might just be a gentle giant.

BUG

The smallest kid at the school, Bug might also be the meanest.

KNUCKLES

The girl with the biggest fists has an even bigger attitude.

DAFT

This girl seems to be on another planet as she is always saying the daftest things.

PONGO

Pongo delights in being the smelliest kid in the whole school – if not the entire world. Everywhere he goes, Pongo is followed around by a stinky brown cloud.

BOOM

Boom is a girl who has always got something to say, and she says it REALLY LOUDLY!

DOCTOR DOKTUR

The mysterious birdlike Science teacher at **THE CRUEL SCHOOL** has beady eyes, a beaky nose and her cape flutters behind her like wings. Doctor Doktur inspires terror in all the children. Any pupil who is sent to one of her detentions is never the same again.

GRUNT

Doctor Doktur's laboratory assistant speaks only in grunts. "HURR!" One grunt for yes. Two for no. Any more than that and nobody has a clue what he is saying. Not even him. Grunt is completely bald but wears the most extraordinary wig. The wig is a one-legged cat named Fiend that crouches on top of his head.

MEDDLE

The spooky caretaker is tall and wide, with a beard that goes down to his belly button. Meddle has the hugest jumbles of keys on his belt.

PROFESSOR DOKTUR

Professor Doktur is Doctor Doktur's elderly mother. She has been the headmistress of **THE CRUEL SCHOOL** for as long as anyone can remember, but the strange thing is that no one has seen her for years. Some think that the professor mysteriously disappeared from the school many years ago.

RANK

Rank is the school dinner lady from your worst nightmares. She prides herself on serving up food that children can't keep down.

MISS DUNK

THE CRUEL SCHOOL librarian is infinitely more interested in biscuits than books.

MISS CLOMP

Clomp is the horrible teacher from
Larker's original school. She hates
Larker with all her heart.

THE BOATMAN

The boatman is the mysterious hooded figure who
transports children from the mainland to the volcanic
island where **THE CRUEL SCHOOL** is situated.

DIGITS

The Maths teacher has a metal hand with six fingers on it. Digits has eleven digits in total, but he thinks he only has ten. So, when Digits counts on his fingers to solve a Maths question, he is always wrong. It is a pity for his poor pupils, who have zero chance of getting an answer right.

MR BLACK

The Art teacher, with black hair, a black goatee beard and all-black clothes, demands his pupils only paint in black.

MISS BALL

The Sports teacher's games are so rough that afterwards her pupils are sent straight to the sick bay.

MR BUSH

The bearded Geography teacher likes to bring the dangers of the outside world inside his classroom.

MISS GIBBER

The teacher takes classes in a language that she herself invented, called Gabber. The problem is that Gabber is utter nonsense and completely impossible to understand. Any child taking a test in Gabber is doomed to failure.

And last but not least…

WORMS

The grubby gardener is nicknamed "Worms" as he always has worms in his pocket. He spends most of his time pottering in his shed, talking to no one except his worms. He has spent his entire life at **THE CRUEL SCHOOL**, having been a pupil there before he became the gardener.

⊱ THE BEASTS ⊰

FIEND

The evillest cat that ever lived, Fiend has only one eye and one leg. However, on the end of that leg is a paw with the longest, sharpest, deadliest claws you ever did see, and she is not afraid to use it. Fiend lives on top of Grunt's bald head.

SQUAWK

Squawk is a pelican that is chained to the tallest turret on the castle that is **THE CRUEL SCHOOL**. The pelican is a replacement for the school bell that broke many years ago. The bird squawks to signal the beginning and end of the school day.

WORMY

Wormy is Worms's imaginatively named pet worm.

And finally...

...the

MEGAMONSTER!*

* This creature will remain a mystery, for now…

Chapter 1
LARKER

Many years ago, in a land far away from our own, a long wooden jetty reached out to sea. Our adventure begins one night so still it was eerie. The only light was that of the moon, the only sound the lapping of waves against the jetty.

Standing on the jetty, silhouetted by the moon, were two figures looking out to sea. One was short. The other was tall.

The short one was a child.

The girl was short for her age, but always got noticed for her magnificently cheeky *grin*. She was wearing an ancient duffel coat over her torn school uniform. Her boots had holes in them. So many holes, in fact, that it would be easier to say the holes had boots in them. She was an orphan.

The girl's name was Larker. It wasn't her real name, but everyone called her Larker, so I will too. Larker was nicknamed "Larker" because she was always larking about.

"Why did the octopus blush?" she asked, a *smile* creeping across her face.

"Not another of your silly jokes, Larker. I hoped you would have learned your lesson!" barked the grown-up. She was the tall one, a teacher by the name of Miss Clomp. Clomp clamped a monocle on to her eye. She had a hairstyle that looked as if it had been created with a pudding bowl and a pair of scissors.

"The octopus blushed because it saw the bottom of the ocean!"

"That's not funny!" sneered Clomp.

"I think you will find any joke is funny if it includes the word 'bottom'!"

"I FORBID YOU FROM SAYING THE WORD 'BOTTOM'!"

"'Bottom'?" asked Larker, her face beaming with a cheeky grin.

"YES! 'BOTTOM'!"

"But, miss, you just said 'bottom'!"

"Yes, I said 'bottom' but only to tell you not to say 'bottom'!"

"You just said 'bottom' twice!"

"STOP SAYING 'BOTTOM'!" said Clomp, stamping her foot in frustration.

STOMP!

The rotten wooden beams on the jetty creaked under her.

CREAK!

To steady herself, Clomp slammed her hand down hard on the girl's shoulder.

THUMP!

"Miss?"

"What now?"

"What's the difference between teachers and sweets?"

"I don't know and I don't care!"

"Children like sweets!"

"PUT A SOCK IN IT!"

"My mum and dad taught me that you have to *laugh,* even in the worst of times."

"Well, they aren't here, are they? So not another word!"

Larker bowed her head sorrowfully. Every day, her heart ached because her parents were gone forever. That's why she loved cracking jokes all the time. She knew sadness and didn't want others to feel sad too. It made her happy to make other people happy.

Just then a long wooden rowing boat emerged from the fog that draped over the water like a ghostly curtain.

"Aha! Right on time," said Clomp, checking her watch. "Every night at midnight, the **CRUEL SCHOOL** boat comes to collect the latest naughty child."

Rowing the boat was a mysterious hooded figure.

Larker gasped.

"Frightened, are you?" purred Clomp.

"No, no!" lied Larker. "Just feeling **burptastic.**" Then she forced out a little burp. **"BURP!** That's got it!" she added, thumping her chest. "No, I am really looking forward to it. I can't wait! **THE CRUEL SCHOOL!** It sounds such fun! Just one tiny thing?"

"Yes?"

"Erm, will I be there long?"

Clomp grinned ghoulishly. **"Just the rest of your life!"**

Chapter 2
THE LAST LAUGH

"I beg your pardon, Miss Clomp!" spluttered Larker. "I think you said I would be there for the rest of my life, and I am planning to live for a long time!"

"The naughty children used to come back from **THE CRUEL SCHOOL** when they weren't naughty any more," replied the wicked teacher. "But now no one ever leaves."

"I will have to **escape**, then!"

"**Escape** is impossible."

"Nothing is impossible!" said Larker.

At that moment, the **CRUEL SCHOOL** boat arrived at the end of the jetty. The hooded figure onboard threw a rope out to Miss Clomp. The teacher caught the end and tied it to the jetty. Then the mysterious figure held out his long, bony fingers and grabbed Larker's wrist. The boatman's fingers were strangely cold to the touch.

Thoughts flashed through Larker's mind of making a run for it, or even a swim for it. But now, with both of Clomp's hands on her shoulders guiding her into the boat, it was hopeless.

Larker had never been on a boat before, and immediately felt ill at ease as it rocked to and fro. This feeling of deep unease wasn't helped by the fact that the boatman's face remained hidden under the hood. A long, bony finger gestured for the girl to sit at the bow of the boat.

"So long, Larker!" scoffed Clomp from the jetty. "This is what happens to naughty children who put whoopee cushions on the headmistress's chair!"

"For the last time, miss, it wasn't me!"

"I know!" replied the teacher with a smirk.

"How do you know?"

"Because it was my whoopee cushion!" chirped Clomp, holding up the little red balloon.

"CLOMP!" screamed the girl. "WHY?"

"I wanted you and your larks banished from our school forever!"

"BUT—"

"This time, I will have the last laugh."

With that, Clomp squeezed the whoopee cushion and it made its naughty noise.

PFFFT!

"HA! HA!" laughed Clomp. "You got the blame!"

The boatman gestured for the rope to be untied from the jetty.

"Let me!" chirped Larker, her eyes flashing with mischief. She fiddled with the rope before calling out, "All done! And, Miss Clomp?"

"Yes?"

"I always have the last laugh."

The boatman began rowing away, but the rope was still attached. It yanked hard on the jetty.

YANK!

The jetty broke.

SNAP!

And collapsed into the sea.

SPLOSH!

It took Miss Clomp with it, plunging her into the cold water.

SPLOOOSH!

"ARGH!" she cried as she began to scramble back on to the collapsed jetty.

"HA! HA! I told you so!" hooted Larker.

The boatman seemed unmoved by all this and continued rowing out into the inky sea.

In no time, the mainland disappeared into the thick fog.

A shiver slithered down the girl's back. Was she going to be at **THE CRUEL SCHOOL** forever? She had to **escape**.

Larker had never learned to swim, but she was prepared to risk it. Now was the time!

The longer she left it, the further she would have to swim back to the land.

Her heart was racing.

BOOM! BOOM! BOOM!

She leaped to her feet and then leaped off the boat into the sea.

SPLOSH!

"URGH!" she gasped in shock at hitting the freezing-cold water.

Frantically, Larker began doggy-paddling away from the boat in what she hoped would be the direction of the jetty.

However, she'd barely had time to thrash around, drowning, when she noticed something powering through the water, heading straight towards her.

Larker recognised that fin.

It could only be one thing.

A shark!

Chapter 3
CIRCLING FINS

Larker spun round in the sea, desperate to speed back to the boat.

"HELP!" she cried, which was a bit rich as she was the one who'd just leaped into the sea.

However, between her and the boat was another shark. And another! And another!

Fins were circling the girl. Any moment now, she was about to become SHARK FOOD!

"HEEELLP!" she cried again as she felt another huge beast brushing past her legs.

Larker shut her eyes tight.

Next, she felt something hard prodding her arm.

She didn't dare open her eyes! It must be the nose of a shark! It prodded again. Larker opened one eye. It was the end of an oar! The mysterious boatman was trying to rescue her. Larker held on tight as she was dragged through the water, sharks snapping at her heels.

SNAP! SNAP! SNAP!
SWOOSH!

When she reached the side of the boat, the figure hauled her on board, but not before the biggest and seemingly hungriest of the sharks had sunk its razor-sharp teeth into her duffel coat.

MUNCH!

Larker ended up in a soaking-wet heap in the boat, while the coat disappeared under the waves.

"I never did like that duffel coat!" she joked.

Needless to say, the boatman didn't laugh. Or giggle. Or even snort.

Larker slumped back down on the bench in her cold, wet clothes.

The boatman rowed on through the fog as the sharks fought over the coat.

"Who knew sharks liked the taste of duffel?"

Still nothing.

"Come on! That was funny! You are one tough crowd, Mr Boatman. Got another one for you. What did the shark say after eating a clownfish? That tasted a little funny! No? Got another one. How did the hammerhead do in his test? He nailed it! What happens when you mix a shark and a cow together? I don't know, but I wouldn't want to milk it! Come on! These are gold!"

The boatman did not respond in any way and continued rowing in perfect rhythm.

Larker sat there trying to enjoy the view of the fog.

As she listened, she could swear she heard the sound of ticking and whirring – like a clock, but louder.

TICK TOCK TICK TOCK!

"Can you hear that?" she asked, then shook her head. There was no way she was going to get an answer out of him. "Never mind. Wake me up when we get to the funfair!"

Larker closed her eyes and pretended to sleep. Suddenly she felt a terrible chill. A wicked wind had whipped up. She opened her eyes to black clouds rolling low over the sea. Then lightning struck a stone's throw from the boat.

CRACKLE!

A rumble of thunder followed.

BOOM!

Waves began to swell, rocking the rowing boat as if it were some deadly fairground ride.

Larker clung on desperately, her grimy fingernails digging into the wood.

The boatman didn't break his rhythm. Instead, the figure continued rowing as buckets of rain poured down on them, flooding the boat.

Finally, there it was, emerging from the storm.

THE CRUEL SCHOOL.

Chapter 4
THE CRUEL SCHOOL

The silhouette of a castle stood on a huge black volcanic rock jutting out of the sea. The castle looked as if it had been randomly added to over the centuries: it was a muddle of towers and turrets. It was Gothic in style, looking as if it could be home to a family of vampires. But **THE CRUEL SCHOOL** was home to a very different type of monster.

The world's naughtiest children.

Larker was not one of them. She knew the difference between wrong and right. Silly jokes are not a crime. Now she was about to find herself living side by side with the naughtiest of the naughtiest. These kids were going to be absolute HORRORS!

The boatman tied up the boat to a rock, and Larker scoured the island for some steps that might take her up to the castle. There were none. Instead, the world's longest rope ladder dangled down.

The boatman gestured for Larker to climb the ladder. The waves were lashing against the rocks, causing explosions of spray.

SPLOOSH!

"If you say so!" she said, leaping on to the ladder. She clung on for dear life.

C R E A K !

The ancient rope sagged under her weight. Her sodden clothes made her twice as heavy as normal.

SNAP! SNAP! SNAP!

Looking down into the sea, she saw sharks snapping at her ankles. Were these the same sharks or different sharks? There just wasn't time to ask, so she continued climbing the ladder, hauling herself up step by step. Soon the sharks were a long way down.

However, halfway up,

DISASTER STRUCK!

Her wet boots slipped on one of the rungs.

SLIP!

"ARGH!" cried Larker as she tumbled through the air.

WHOOSH!

She just managed to grab hold of the last rung as a giant shark reared out of the water and launched itself at her, jaws wide.

CHOMP!

Despite her exhaustion, having a shark about to eat her gave the girl a sudden burst of energy. Now she raced up the rope ladder as if her life depended on it. Which it did!

CLUNK! CLUNK! CLUNK!

In no time, she reached the top. Larker kissed the cold, wet ground, such was her relief to have not been eaten alive. However, as she looked up, she saw two steel-toecapped boots at eye level.

"Welcome to **THE CRUEL SCHOOL,**" said a voice. "We hope you have an unpleasant stay."

Chapter 5
MEDDLE

"**G**ET UP!" came a bark.

Larker scrambled to her feet. At first, she thought she might still be on her knees as she was only waist height with the figure. But no – this person really was that tall. Larker's face was level with **huge** sets of keys dangling from a thick leather belt. The keys swung forward as the figure straightened up and bashed Larker – **BANG!** – on the nose.

CLANK!

"OUCH! Are you a piano?" asked Larker.

The hulk of a man shook his head. "No! Why would you ask that?"

"You have eighty-eight keys!"

"So, you're the one who put the whoopee cushion on her headmistress's chair!"

He was big and beefy enough to be a circus strongman. The man had the appearance of a cupboard that had been stuffed into overalls. To add to his startling look, he had a long, scruffy beard that went all the way down to his belly button. The castle loomed behind him as if it were his own enormous shadow.

"It wasn't me!" protested Larker.

"That's what they all say," mocked the man.

"It was my teacher who did it!"

"A likely story! I am the caretaker, Meddle."

"I've got a joke for you."

"I don't want to hear it."

"What do caretakers do at night? They go to sweep!"

"That's not funny!"

There it was again! That strange ticking sound Larker had heard on the boat.

TICK TOCK TICK TOCK!

"What's that?" she asked.

"What's what?"

"That!"

"What's that?"

"Listen. Can't you hear ticking?"

TICK TOCK TICK TOCK!

No one said a word, before Meddle replied firmly, "NO! First sign you are going bananas: hearing things that aren't there."

GGGRRRUUUMMMPPPHHH!

There was a deep, low rumble from beneath. The ground they were standing on shook.

R U M B L E !

"You must have heard that!" exclaimed Larker.

"Oh yes! You are not imagining that."

"What is it?"

"The volcano. It is underneath our feet."

The girl looked down. "Who builds a castle on top of a volcano?"

"The land must have been cheap."

"Even so!"

"Don't you worry. The volcano hasn't erupted for hundreds of years."

"Maybe it is due to!"

"The old girl has a grumble now and again, but it is nothing to worry about. Now, come with me. I will show you to your room," he said with a deep snort.

Meddle led Larker inside the spooky castle, along seemingly endless dark, dank stone passages, illuminated only by the occasional flaming torch. It was now long past midnight, so most of the other children must have been asleep. There was the noise of snoring and trumping echoing along the hallways.

"ZZZZ!"

PFFT!

"ZZZZZ!"

PFFFT!

"ZZZZZZ!"

PFFFFT!

It sounded more like a zoo than a school, and smelled more like one too.

PONGORIA!*

After a while, the pair arrived at a thick wooden door.

The caretaker jangled through his keys until he finally found the right one.

JINGLE! JANGLE!

"I do hope your quarters are to your satisfaction, Your Royal Highness!" said Meddle with another low snort as he opened the heavy door.

It was a cold, sad little room with a straw mattress on the bed and a rusty bucket in the corner.

---

* *A real made-up word you will find in the biggest and best book of words, the trusted* **Walliamsictionary.**

"I love what you've done to the place!" joked Larker.

Meddle frowned. "Cheek like that won't get you anywhere in here. Cheeky ones like you find themselves in DETENTION."

"DETENTION! I got a DETENTION once for making chicken noises!"

"What are you on about now?"

"I was using fowl language! Do you get it?"

"DETENTION here at THE CRUEL SCHOOL is no laughing matter. Children who get DETENTION are never the same again."

Larker was alarmed. "What do you mean?"

"Keep on asking questions like that, Your Royal Highness, and you will find out for yourself. Now sleep tight, and be sure to let the bedbugs bite."

"Let them bite?"

"They will anyway!"

Just a glance at the straw mattress on the bed was enough to see it was alive with creepy-crawlies.

NIP! NIP!

SCRATCH! SCRATCH!

W H I R R! W H I R R!

Larker slumped down on the mattress and immediately began to itch all over. Even her itches had itches!

What's more, her tummy gurgled like the depths of a swamp.

FURZGURGLE!

"The volcano again!" remarked Meddle.

"No. That was my tummy. I'm hungry!"

"It sounds like it!" He snorted again.

"What's so funny about that? Would you like to see me starve?"

"I'd love to, but I don't have the time. Breakfast is at dawn."

"Thank you."

"And it is DISGUSTING!"

The caretaker limped out and the heavy wooden door swung closed.

"Well then, I will just have to **escape**," announced Larker.

"It's impossible."

"Nothing is impossible!"

At that, Meddle disappeared down the passageway, his jumble of keys jangling all the way.

JINGLE! JANGLE! JONGLE!

Larker was more determined than ever that she would find a way out. As a big, filthy rat scampered over her face, she felt **escape** couldn't come **soon enough!**

Chapter 6
SQUAWK!

No sooner had Larker finally drifted off to sleep than she was woken by a deafening sound.

"SQUAWK!"

And again louder.

"SQUAWK!"

And a third time, louder still.

"SQUAWK!"

Larker scrambled up off the straw mattress. She turned the rusty tin bucket upside down and climbed on it so she could peer out of her tiny window.

Dawn was rising over the island. The castle's damp black stone walls were glistening in the low morning light. At the edge of the cliff was an old, battered shed. She could just make out a figure in the shed, staring back at her.

As soon as she spotted it, the figure disappeared from view.

The squawks were coming from a seabird with a huge bill. It was cruelly tied to the top of one of the turrets so it couldn't fly away. The bird was a pelican, and it was being poked to force it to make that sound. Leering out of a hatch further down the roof was Meddle. The caretaker was prodding the poor bird with the end of a mop.

POKE!

"SQUAWK!"

POKE!

"SQUAWK!"

POKE!

"SQUAWK!"

It was clear things were done very differently at **THE CRUEL SCHOOL.** You might expect to be woken up by a cock crowing, or a bell chiming, or a gong being gonged, but no. Not here.

Cruelty was the order of the day, even for a poor pelican.

It was horrid to witness. Larker clearly wasn't the only soul who needed to escape this dreadful place...

Moments later, her door swung open.

C R E A K !

"WAKEY! WAKEY!" shouted Meddle.

"There was a rat in here last night."

"Just the one?"

"Yes. What will a rat never tell you? A squeakret!"

"Well, if you like rats, you're going to love your breakfast. The dining hall is that way!"

Larker followed the direction in which Meddle's finger was pointing. She joined the throng of grubby-looking children elbowing each other out of the way as they stomped down the passageway.

"I HATE YOU!"

"YOU STINK!"

"I'LL STINK YOU!"

It was every child for themselves here at **THE CRUEL SCHOOL.** They had been treated with cruelty by the grown-ups, so – without thought – that was how they treated each other.

Larker kept her head down. As the new girl, the last thing she wanted was to attract any unwanted attention.

"WHO WANTS A DEAD LEG?"

"JUST YOU TRY AND I WILL BASH YOU ON THE BUM!"

"SOMEONE'S GUFFED!"

"PONGO!"

If Larker thought the children were pongy, nothing could prepare her for the evil smell that was about to hit her when she reached the dining hall.

It was like a

WALL OF STINK!

The girl stood dead still. She couldn't take another step – she would choke. Or faint. Or be sick. Or all three at once.

But there were brutish boys and gruesome girls behind her, all clamouring to be fed. Larker found herself being jostled into the dining hall.

"GET OUT OF MY WAY!"

"SILLY GIRL!"

"PUSH HER OVER! TEACH HER A LESSON!"

Once inside the dining hall, Larker pinched her nose, such was the ghastliness of the smell.

But the pong was nothing

compared to what was to come…

the taste!

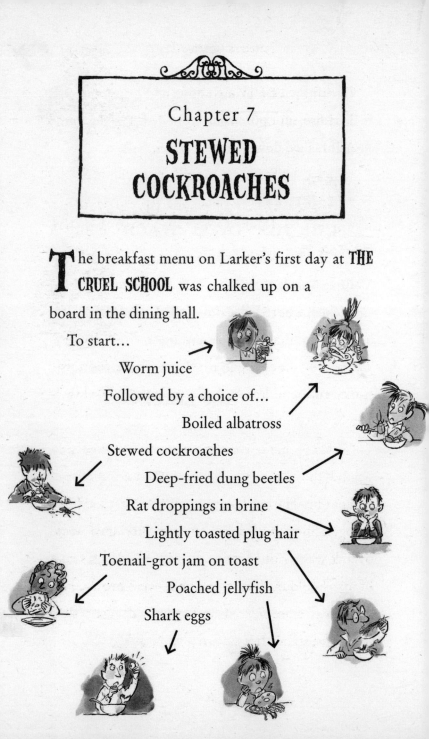

Chapter 7
STEWED COCKROACHES

The breakfast menu on Larker's first day at **THE CRUEL SCHOOL** was chalked up on a board in the dining hall.

To start...

Worm juice

Followed by a choice of...

Boiled albatross

Stewed cockroaches

Deep-fried dung beetles

Rat droppings in brine

Lightly toasted plug hair

Toenail-grot jam on toast

Poached jellyfish

Shark eggs

Or, for the **really** adventurous:

Tortoise-snot porridge!

All washed down with a mug of:

Steaming seagull-dropping tea!

YUCKETY YUCK YUCK YUCK!

With rock cakes to go.

Made from actual rocks!

Larker scoured the counter of horrors. As hungry as she was, there was no way she could eat even a crumb. As the noisy, stinky, rude children pushed past her and filled their bowls, she grimaced.

"WOT?" barked the wizened old dinner lady behind the counter. All her teeth had fallen out except one. The one lonely tooth made her look like an ogre. She sounded like one too. Her once-white overall was a riot of stains. It was like Joseph's coat of many colours, if all the colours were brown. Her name was embroidered on the overall, just visible under the stains. It was, fittingly, "Rank".

"Well, this all looks absolutely delicious, Mrs... er, Rank," began Larker, her voice sounding very peculiar because she was pinching her nose.

"JUST RANK!"

"Rank. And the smell is, well, eye-watering. I've got a joke for you!"

"I hate jokes."

"What do cows have for breakfast? Moosli!"

"I don't get it."

"What do mice have for breakfast? Mice krispies! What do snowmen have for breakfast? Snowflakes! Which makes me wonder if you have any cornflakes, please?"

Larker added a hopeful little smile. Perhaps... perhaps... *perhaps* this might just charm the ogre?

No such luck.

"CORNFLAKES?" repeated Rank. Then she repeated it, louder this time. "CORNFLAKES?"

All the nasty children who were now sitting at the long table, shovelling down their breakfasts, looked up and listened.

"CORNFLAKES?" shouted Rank.

"Yes," replied Larker. "Cornflakes. They're, well, flakes of corn!"

"MISS LAH-DI-DAH 'ERE WANTS CORNFLAKES!

HA! HA! HA!"

Cornflakes didn't seem at all like the kind of breakfast someone who was really posh and lah-di-dah would have, but the other children hooted with laughter.

"HA! HA! HA!"

Larker wished she could disappear when she saw everyone was laughing at her. She adored everyone laughing WITH her – that was the best feeling in the world. But everyone laughing AT her was the worst. For a moment, she was tempted to disappear by diving into the giant vat of seagull-dropping tea. But she thought better of it.

"We don't have precious delicacies like cornflakes here at THE CRUEL SCHOOL!" hooted Rank. "You are here because – just like these scoundrels – you have been badder than bad, remember! This food is all part of the punishment!"

With that, the dinner lady leaned in towards the girl. Once again, Larker could hear that peculiar **ticking** sound she'd heard on the boat and also with Meddle.

"What's that noise?" she asked.

"I can't hear nuffink."

"I can definitely hear something."

Rank smirked and summoned something dark and deadly from the pit of her stomach.

She let off the most deafening belch right in Larker's face. "BURP!"

The stink was enough to sweep Larker off her feet.

"Did you 'ear that?" asked Rank.

"Oh yes. I heard that loud and clear!"

"Good! Now there's one meal a day at **THE CRUEL SCHOOL** and this is it. So take your grub and clear off!"

Rank slopped a giant ladle of porridge into a dirty bowl.

SPLUT!

It splattered all over the girl, covering her from head to toe in tortoise snot.

"OOPS!" said Rank with a smirk, which showed off her one lonely tooth.

Needless to say, this prompted another hoot of

mocking laughter from the children.

"HA! HA! HA!"

Larker sighed. It was only her first morning at **THE CRUEL SCHOOL,** but things

couldn't have got off to a

worse start!

Chapter 8
UNSPEAKABLE CRIMES

Like a silent movie comedian, Larker theatrically wiped the tortoise snot from her eyes.

SPLAT!

SPLUT!

"Never mind *that* burp!" shouted a stinky-looking boy. "Wait until you hear this!"

There followed the sound of the loudest bottom banger you have ever heard.

KABOOM!

All the children hooted with laughter…

"HA! HA! HA!"

…as a cloud of deepest, darkest brown descended upon Larker.

"It's a shame trumping isn't in the Olympics,"

she said, sniffing the air. "Or you would win a gold medal!"

"WHOEVER SMELT IT DEALT IT!" exclaimed the stinky boy.

"WHOEVER SAID THE RHYME DID THE CRIME!" retorted Larker.

"Don't go there!" shouted a girl with hands as big as a giant's feet. "Pongo knows 'em all!"

The duel had begun.

"WHOEVER SANG THE SONG DID THE PONG!" replied Pongo.

"WHOEVER DEDUCED IT PRODUCED IT!" said Larker, enjoying herself.

Pongo thought for a moment and narrowed his eyes. "WHOEVER THUNK IT STUNK IT!"

"He's got you beat!" shouted the huge-handed girl.

Larker thought for a moment. "WHOEVER ARTICULATED IT PARTICULATED IT!"

"Never heard that one before!" exclaimed the girl.

"WHOEVER DOES THE SQUEALING IS CONCEALING!" said Pongo. Judging by the smug look on his face, he was sure there were no more comebacks to come back!

Larker shut her eyes tight as she spun through the encyclopedia of jokes in her head. "WHOEVER SPOKE LAST DELIVERED THE BLAST!"

Pongo thought for a second and shook his head.

"YOU BEAT PONGO!" said the girl.

There was a low cheer from the other kids. Almost like cows mooing.

"WOO!"

"Well, I just need somewhere to sit down," said Larker.

There was a huge hulk of a boy on his own at the far end of the long dining table. He had missing teeth, a broken nose and a cauliflower ear. Without doubt, he

73

looked like he started fights or, more likely, ended them, so Larker thought it best to give him a wide berth.

All the others glowered at the new girl, trying to make her feel as unwelcome as possible.

"You're not sitting next to me!" said Pongo.

"And don't you dare sit 'ere!" added the girl with the huge hands. She thumped the table hard.

T H O N K !

"AND IF YOU SIT HERE THEN THERE'S GONNA BE BIG TROUBLE!" shouted a third. She was clearly the loudest girl at the school as she spoke at ten times the volume of everyone else.

"And you definitely can't sit 'ere as there is no actual room to sit down anyway!" added another girl.

"DAFT!" shouted the girl with the huge hands, slapping her own forehead with frustration at the idiocy. "You're so… DAFT!"

SLAP!

Larker needed her wit now more than ever.

"There would be plenty of room for me to sit down if all your bottoms were not so GINORMOUS!"

"NOOO!" came shouts all over the dining hall. Breakfast began flying through the air. Larker had caused a humongous FOOD FIGHT!

"STOP!" bellowed Rank, just as a wave of worm juice all but swept her off her feet.

SWOOSH!

Stewed cockroaches, shark eggs and poached jellyfish flew through the air.

ZOOM!

WHIZZ!

SPLAT!

Meanwhile, Larker spotted what looked like the littlest kid in the school. Unlike the others, he had neat hair parted in the middle and a thick pair of glasses. He looked harmless enough, so Larker sat down opposite him.

"Hello. I'm Larker!" she chirped. "Are you enjoying your toenail grot on toast?"

"It's disgusting," replied the boy. "But not as disgusting as you!"

With that, he shoved the piece of toast straight into Larker's face.

SPLOT!

"SHOULD HAVE DONE IT HARDER, BUG!" shouted the loudest girl.

"Shut your face, Boom!" came the reply.

Once again, all the children hooted with laughter at the new girl with a face full of toenail-grot jam.

"HA! HA! HA!"

Larker had just discovered that even the littlest kid in the school was a HUGE HORROR!

All these children had been sent to **THE CRUEL SCHOOL** for the most unspeakable crimes:

Bug had put bottom-burp powder in his

headmaster's coffee on a speech day.

PFFT!

The girl with the huge hands –
Knuckles – had flattened
her entire school
with a stolen
steamroller.

CRRRRUUUNNNCCCHHH!

Daft had put live piranhas down the
bowls of the teachers' toilets.

SNAP! SNAP! SNAP! SNAP! SNAP!
"YIKES!"

On a deadly dull day out to a boring
old medieval fort, the colossal
boy – Spod – had catapulted his History
teacher into the next county.

WHIZZ!

Pongo had stolen the "L" from the school sign, which read: POOL HERE.

"TEE! HEE!"

When her elderly Geography teacher nodded off in class, Boom woke him up by playing a trumpet in his ear.

BROO-DOO-DOO!

The food fight had ended. For now. There was nothing left to hurl. But still the hoots of laughter kept coming at Larker.

"HA! HA! HA!"

"Look at her silly face!"

"Serves her right!"

Scouring the dining hall, she spotted someone who was not laughing. It was the hulk of a boy at the far end of the table. All this time, he'd been minding his own business, scoffing away, ignoring the mayhem around him. Even when a jellyfish landed on his head, he just shovelled another whole shark egg into his gob.

GULP!

So Larker took her chances and moved places to sit opposite him.

"I seem to have missed my mouth entirely," she joked, pointing at the toenail-grot jam stuck to her face.

The boy didn't react.

Larker sighed and twirled the tortoise snot around in her bowl with her spoon.

TWIZZLE!

The porridge was luminous green and looked like slime from another solar system. She sniffed it.

PONGY WONGY WOO WAH!

Despite being deliriously hungry, there was no way she was going to eat that. In frustration, Larker slammed her spoon down on the table.

CLUNK!

The noise caused the boy to look up.

"Can I have your porridge?" he asked politely while shoving food into his mouth.

GULP!

Is he bananas? thought Larker.

"Be my guest!" she replied. She couldn't be more delighted to offload her disgusting tortoise-snot porridge on someone else.

"Are you sure? We don't get fed again until tomorrow!"

"I am sure!"

"Fanks!" replied the boy,

going to work on her bowl.

Chapter 9
SPOD

As they sat in **THE CRUEL SCHOOL** dining hall, Larker looked on in amazement at Spod finishing the bowl of snot in seconds.

"YUM!" he exclaimed.

"Yum?" repeated Larker, incredulous.

"You get used to the taste of tortoise snot after a while!"

"I'm not sure I ever will."

"It takes away the taste of the shark eggs."

"I will take your word for it. Hey, I've got a gag for you. I had a great teacher at my last school called Mr Turtle. He tortoise well!"

The boy was silent.

"Do you get it?" asked Larker.

"Dunno!"

"Don't worry. So how long have you been here?"

"**Dunno.** Years, I guess. I don't remember life outside this place."

"But you must have a family who are missing you."

"**Dunno.**"

"Why is the answer to every question '**dunno**'?"

The boy looked lost in thought for a moment before replying, "**Dunno.**"

"Don't tell me your name is '**Dunno**'!" she joked.

"Nah! It's Spod."

"Spod! Why are you called Spod?"

"**Dunno.**"

"I should have known," she replied.

"It's just that everyone calls me that."

Larker leaned in to speak to the boy in confidence.

"So, are you planning to stay here forever?"

"**Dunno.**"

"Only, I am planning to get out of here. Are you in?"

"**Dunno?**"

"What do you mean, '**dunno**'?"

"**Dunno** where else I would go. Kids like me don't fit in nowhere."

At that moment, there was another deafening SQUAWK.

"SQUAWK!"

It was the pelican again!

Immediately, all the children got up from the table.

"What's going on?" asked Larker. "And don't say '**dunno**'!"

"That sound means it's time for the first torture, I mean *lesson*, of the day."

Spod stood up, taking his plate with him, so Larker followed. However, as this was her first day and she didn't know the school rules yet, she put her empty bowl in the wrong place. She put it on top of a pile of plates.

If there was one thing guaranteed to send Rank into a spiral of rage, it was either a bowl stacked on the stack of plates or a plate stacked on the stack of bowls.

"The bowls don't go **there!**" yelled the old woman.

"I'm so sorry!" replied Larker.

"How dare you make more work for me!"

"Well, I er…"

But before Larker could say another thing she felt a bowl skim past the top of her head…

WHOOSH!

...and explode against the wall behind her.

KABOOM!

"Nasty, selfish little beasts like you need to be taught a lesson!" thundered Rank.

She picked up the stack of plates and hurled them one by one at Larker.

W H O O S H !

WHOOSH! WHOOSH!

KABOOM! KABOOM! KABOOM!

Spod grabbed Larker by the arm.

"I'LL HAVE YOU PUT IN DETENTION, MISSY! SEE HOW YOU LIKE THAT!"

"You don't want to be put in DETENTION! Trust me!" hissed Spod to Larker. "Let's make a run for it before Rank gets in a bad mood."

"This isn't a bad mood?" exclaimed Larker in disbelief as more and more plates exploded around her.

WHOOSH! WHOOSH!

WHOOSH!

WHOOSH! WHOOSH! WHOOSH!

KABOOM! KABOOM! KABOOM! KABOOM! KABOOM!

"This school is POTTY!" said Larker.

"Oh, you don't know the half of it! Just wait until our first lesson! Follow me!"

He grabbed the girl by the hand and led her out of the dining hall as a hail of plates smashed against the door.

KABOOM! KABOOM! KABOOM! KABOOM! KABOOM!

Chapter 10
DIGITS

Maths can be hard enough at the best of times, but, if your teacher cannot count, it becomes IMPOSSIBLE.

Let me explain.

The Maths teacher at **THE CRUEL SCHOOL** was called Digits. Digits sported a heavy tweed three-piece suit with a bow tie. He had a wild shock of grey hair that went up to the ceiling and a long, straggly beard that went down to the floor.

What was most memorable about Digits, however, was that one of his hands was made of metal. The metal hand had six fingers on it. That meant the teacher had eleven fingers in total – but Digits thought he only had ten.

So whenever he counted on his fingers to solve a

Maths question he always got the answer WRONG.

Larker was something of a whizz when it came to Maths. She was one of those kids who could take one look at a bag of marbles or a box of matches or a pile of coins and tell you in an instant how many there were. So when Digits started chalking away on the blackboard in the chilly stone classroom and announced, "Seventeen thousand, four hundred and fifty-six minus eleven. You have ten seconds to answer the question. Ten…" he was not expecting the new girl to put her hand up before he'd had the chance to say "nine".

"I've got it, sir!" she exclaimed.

The kids in the class all looked at her in disbelief.

"I beg your pardon?" spluttered the teacher.

"I've got the answer, sir."

Digits let out a weary sigh. "No child has ever got the answer to one of my questions right in the fifty years I have been teaching Maths here at **THE CRUEL SCHOOL**."

"Well, I have!" announced Larker proudly.

From the desk behind, Spod coughed to get her attention.

"AHEM!"

But she took no notice.

"The answer is, wait for it…" she teased.

"Out with it!" thundered Digits, throwing a piece of chalk at her head.

WHIZZ!

Fortunately, she ducked just in time.

The chalk hit Spod on the chin…

CRACK!

…and exploded into dust.

WHOOSH!

"DRUM ROLL, PLEASE!" announced Larker.

This time, Digits threw the board eraser at her. Once again, she ducked, and once again it hit Spod.

DOINK!

It bounced off his forehead, and the hulk of a boy didn't even blink.

"Seventeen thousand, four hundred and forty-five!" she said, folding her arms neatly together and looking outrageously SMUG.

"You sound very confident!" chuckled Digits. "Let's all see, shall we?"

Digits then opened his hands to count on his fingers. "Ten fingers, this will be simple!"

All the children in his class sighed. They had been here a thousand times before. Or, according to Digits, a thousand and one times before.

So the eleven-digited teacher counted down from 17,456 on his fingers. Needless

TICK TOCK   TICK TOCK

90

to say, the answer he came to was, "Seventeen thousand, four hundred and forty-four!"

Digits paced over to this new girl and leaned on her desk so he was face to face with her.

"What a shame, Little Miss Clever Clogs! You are wrong, wrong, WRONG!"

TICK TOCK TICK TOCK!

There was that sound again.

"I can hear something strange," she said softly.

Immediately, Digits marched back to the front of the class. He picked up a heavy Maths textbook from his desk and, with all his might, hurled it at Larker.

WHIZZ!

She ducked once again, and it hit Spod bang on the nose.

BOINK!

"No matter, Spod," said Digits. "Fortunately, your nose is already broken!"

"Yes, sir. Thank you, sir," replied the boy.

"Look, sir! I got the answer right, sir!" protested Larker.

A hush descended on the classroom. No one had ever dared challenge Digits before.

This felt like the

start of something!

Could it be the

beginning of a...

REVOLUTION?

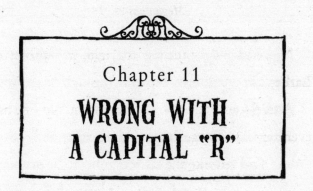

Chapter 11
WRONG WITH A CAPITAL "R"

Up until now, few of the children in the Maths class had been listening.

Knuckles had been plucking earwax out of her ears with her pencil.

P L O P !

Boom had been creating snowstorms with her dandruff.

WHOOSH!

Daft had been lying in a pool of her own dribble on her desk.

ZZZZ!

Pongo had been letting off bottom bangers into his cupped hand before wafting them to his next-door neighbour.

PFFT!

Bug had been creating the biggest bubbles of runny snot possible by blowing through one nostril.

GURGLE!

After Larker's challenge to the teacher, they all sat up and paid attention. This was going to be exciting!

No one ever took on Digits. Digits was a hurler, and you never knew what he was going to hurl at you next. Once, he even hurled Pongo right at Spod.

Was this new girl going to get the better of the terrible teacher on her very first day at

THE CRUEL SCHOOL?

"*I was right, sir!*" mocked Digits. He picked up a chair and hurled it across the classroom.

W H I Z Z !

Fortunately, everyone ducked, and it smashed against the back wall.

CRASH!

"Look what you've done now, girl!" thundered Digits. "You've broken the chair!"

"I didn't break it. You threw it!"

"Yes, but if it had hit you it wouldn't have broken."

"Digits has a point!" agreed Boom.

"You were wrong!" declared Digits. "Wrong! Wrong! Wrong! Wrong with a capital 'R'! WRONG!"

"Spelling isn't your strong suit, then," murmured Larker.

"What did you just say?" demanded Digits.

"Nothing, sir!" she chirped.

"I will prove you wrong! Didn't you see me

95

count on my fingers?"

There was a collective gasp from the class.

"GASP!"

Spod glared at the girl as if to say, "DON'T!"

"Yes, I did, sir!" replied Larker. "And you counted one too many."

"How, pray, would I have done that?" he demanded. "I have ten fingers!"

"No, you don't. You have eleven!"

"GASP!" went everyone.

Spod did a double gasp to really get the point across to Larker. "GASP! GASP!"

Digits was in a TERRIBLE TEMPER! With some difficulty, he picked up his desk before hurling it across the room.

WHIZZ!

Larker ducked, but it hit Spod on the head.

BASH!

The desk exploded into pieces, sending shards of wood flying everywhere.

WHIZZ!
BANG! WALLOP!

"Are you all right, Spod?" asked Larker.

"Dunno," he replied, rubbing his head.

"This swine thinks I have eleven fingers! Eleven! What rot!" thundered Digits as he counted his eleven fingers again. "One, two, three, four, five, six, seven, eight, nine, ten! See! Just like I have ten toes!"

With that, Digits whipped off his shoes and socks to reveal... a metal foot! The metal foot had – you guessed it – six toes! Just like his fingers, Digits had eleven toes. He counted them.

"One, two, three, four, five, six, seven, eight, nine, ten! And you, Little Miss Clever Clogs, can do ten Maths tests!"

"Shouldn't that be eleven?" asked Larker.

Spod furiously shook his head.

"You can do eleven Maths tests!" exclaimed Digits.

"See, you can count, after all!" muttered the girl, to the great amusement of all the other children.

"HA! HA! HA!"

Now they were laughing with her and not at her. It was the BEST feeling in the world.

"What was that?" demanded Digits.

"Nothing, sir!" she replied with the smuggest of smug grins.

"Why, I should put you in DETEN—"

But before Digits could say "TION" Larker was saved by the bell. Well, not the bell exactly, but the sound of the pelican squawking.

"SQUAWK!"

"That squawk is a signal for me, not you!" shouted Digits, but it was too late – all the kids swarmed out of the classroom as if they were rats escaping a sinking ship.

"No one has ever done anything like that before, Larker," said an excited Spod.

"It was fun!" she replied.

"You're lucky you didn't get a DETENTION."

"I don't care."

"You will care. Kids who get DETENTIONS are never the same again."

"What do you mean?" asked Larker.

"Dunno. I said too much."

"You haven't said enough…"

"The Science teacher always takes the DETENTION. The kids come out zomb-☉-fied!"

Larker stopped in the chilly hallway.

"zomb-☉-fied? Why?"

"Dunno. Nobody knows."

"There are lots of us kids here – why don't you all stand up to the teachers?"

Spod shook his head. "Dunno. I guess we're all out for ourselves here at THE CRUEL SCHOOL."

"But if we all worked together…?" she reasoned.

"It's impossible."

"Nothing's impossible!" said Larker.

"It is. All us kids hate each other."

"I don't hate you."

"I don't hate you either!"

"Well, there's a start!"

The pair shared a *smile*.

"We've already got two!" continued Larker. "Let's join forces and get out of this place forever!"

Spod thought for a moment. "Talk like that gets you in DETENTION. As does being late for your lesson. Come on!"

With that, he took Larker by the hand and yanked her along to the

next classroom.

Chapter 12
GIBBER GABBER

You might expect the children of **THE CRUEL SCHOOL** to be learning a foreign language they could use in later life, such as French or German or Spanish or Mandarin or Russian.

Oh no.

The language teacher, Miss Gibber, taught an entirely made-up language – one that she had made up herself. It was called Gabber. Gabber was absolute nonsense. It was impossible to learn as it kept changing all the time. That was because Gibber could never remember what meaning she might have given to one of her made-up words.

For example, one day Gabber for "spoon" might be "bimmybammy"; the next it might be "furg".

Similarly, the word for "queen" in Gabber might

one day be "spooglefish", the next "fibblyfobblyfoo".

Or the translation of "tree" into Gabber might change from "bumruttock" to "moogymoogymoogy" to "zingleid".

It was impossible to follow, not least for Gibber herself.

Spod managed to give Larker the heads-up on all this just before Gibber waltzed into the classroom.

Gibber was a short lady whose mismatched clothes and glasses made sure she was always noticed.

"Gabber exam today, boys and girls!" she announced as she handed out the papers to a collective groan from the class.

"RUBBISH!" boomed Boom.

"It's not 'rubbish', Boom. All you have to do is translate from Gabber into English! It couldn't be simpler!"

"Have we learned to speak English yet, miss?" asked Daft.

"You are funny, Daft!" said Larker.

"I'm not trying to be," replied the bemused girl.

"Oh!" said Larker as she scanned the exam paper.

The list of words in Gabber was long:

EXAMINATION PAPER ONE

NAME: CLASS:

Doogledangers ....

Grintynookle ....

Yickidy-click ....

Spamfamdam ....

Soosugeberry ....

Bumbumbum ....

Hooheehoohaa ....

Pomtomolom ....

Oooooooooooooooooooooooooooooooooooooooooooooooooooooooooooooooooooooooooooooooooooooooooooooo

Nickynackynoo ....

Qumdumtious ....

Winkleplonk ....

Frink ....

Flobberdobberish ....

Mantypants ....

Eeeeeeeeeeeeeeeeeeeeck ....

Spolondorous ....

Fruntybunt ....

Krimpledongers ....
Dee-doo-dungleberry ....
Woozleplop ....
Yankeldomp ....
Ploo ....
Froobiedicious ....
Splitsplatsplut ....
Woo-waa ....
Quentickle ....
Fonkle ....
Donkle ....
Ponkle ....
Podiousnessnessness ....

SCORE [ ]

"Gibber wants us all to fail," hissed Spod.

"Why?" asked Larker.

"So she can put the lot of us in DETENTION!"

"Not DETENTION!" whispered Pongo.

"We'll never be the same again!" added Bug, mopping his brow nervously. "I was there yesterday, and I feel like I'm burning up. Like I'm going to explode!"

Larker thought for a moment. P I N G ! "I've got an idea! I'm going to beat Gibber at her own game!"

"How?" asked Spod.

"Yeah, how?" joined in Bug, as if he too wanted to be part of the gang.

Larker smiled. "Talk only in Gabber!"

Chapter 13
GING-GANG-GOOLIFIED!

"The Gabber exam begins..." announced Gibber, looking at her watch that ran backwards, "NOW!"

Immediately, Larker popped her hand into the air.

"The exam has started!" huffed the teacher.

"I know, Miss Gibber, but do you mind if I speak to you in Gabber for a moment?"

"In Gabber?" asked a panicked Gibber.

"Yes!"

"Well, I'm not sure..."

"This is a Gabber lesson, isn't it?"

"Of course! Gibber's Gabber!"

"Then what better way to learn the language than to speak it?"

Larker had Gibber cornered. There was no way

out. She had to agree. "Go on, then!"

A mischievous grin spread across Larker's face. This was going to be FUN! Or, to translate "fun" into Gabber, "donkydoodahwhizzyplops"!

Larker began: "Moondongaga bish furlurpably, dockynocky oodabababilly nishquot, gruntlefunk moonlick meekymoo zob zob zob, foobledingdong?"

She ended the sentence with an upwards inflection as if it were a question. But because she had made up this Gabber, just like Gibber did, it was impossible to answer.

For once, Gibber looked dumbstruck.*

Spod's eyes and the eyes of all the other children in the classroom turned to the teacher.

Gibber looked mightily confused. "Erm, please could you repeat the question?"

As is customary in Gabber, now the exact same words were completely different! "Poopah dingaling moogelberry nonton kroonflip mickmackymoo plugrot furgle durgle purgle, groogo obi wuntle hinkylink, broohahahahahahaha?"

Daft, especially, was loving it and joined in the fun. "Moopy fizzfazz mungledrop oodoodoo wimplemuppet zonkydonk! I can speak Gabber!"

"Nice one, Daft!" exclaimed Larker. "Everyone join in!"

Then all the other kids in the class started shouting out their own made-up words too!

"Ploomfizz!"

"Quinickers!"

"Oojelwomp!"

---

* Or, to translate "dumbstruck" into Gabber: ging-gang-goolified!

"Sockypockypoohpah!"

"Fintibulous!"

"Hugrot!"

"Wigglewoggle!"

"Snippysnappysnuppy!"

"Dongleflook!"

"Woogermints!"

"SILENCE!" shouted Gibber. "All of you! You should be ashamed! I've never seen such insolence from a class at **THE CRUEL SCHOOL**!"

Larker popped her hand in the air and immediately started talking. "But you haven't answered my question, miss!" Then she returned to making up silly word after silly word after silly word. "Plimplan hujajaja wooobie wooobie gruntlefumpkin broopienuts pahpahpahpahpapapapa soodlecow drunkle funkle droopledangles quiggle quoggle quaggle willywollywhoo brumstink groggle scudfurp tinky tanky tonk plishplashplosh hoogle briddly bruddly broo, wickledickledungleploop?"

All the children were staring straight at Gibber. Sweat began beading on her forehead. She pulled out a spotty silk handkerchief and dabbed her brow.

"Repeat the question, you nasty little troublemaker! This time NOT in Gabber!" demanded Gibber.

"What I said was," began Larker, a mischievous glint growing in her eyes, "you don't know a word of Gabber, do you, Miss Gibber?"

The children erupted into laughter.

"HA! HA! HA!"

"I like this new girl!" exclaimed Knuckles.

"ME TOO!" agreed Boom.

"She's cool!" added Pongo.

"Who's the new girl again?" asked Daft.

Gibber was so furious she looked as if she were about to COMBUST! She stomped over to Larker's desk. As soon as she got close, the girl could hear that peculiar ticking sound again.

TICK TOCK TICK TOCK!

"GET OUT!" yelled Gibber. "GET OUT OF MY CLASSROOM AT ONCE!"

"Please could you translate that into Gabber?" joked Larker.

"HA! HA! HA!" hooted the children.

"NICE ONE, Larker!" called out Spod.

"SPOD! DETENTION!"

"NOOOOO!" he screamed.

"DOUBLE DETENTION!"

"Sorry, Spod," whispered Larker. She felt awful for landing her only friend at the school in deep DOO-DOO!

"AND AS FOR YOU, LARKER –" screamed the teacher – "GET OUT OF MY CLASSROOM AT ONCE! YOU ARE IN TRIPLE DETEN–"

But before Gibber could say "TION!" Larker waltzed out of the door and slammed it behind her.

BANG!

Chapter 14
AVALANCHE!

Delighted by her own cheekiness at dodging the triple DETENTION, Larker did a little dance along the long stone hallway. Then she felt a pang of guilt about Spod. If what he said about being sent to DETENTION were true, she feared for her friend. What would happen to him there?

Next, echoing in the distance, Larker heard that jingle jangle of keys.

JINGLE! JANGLE! JONGLE!

Oh no!

Meddle was heading her way. The girl hid behind a suit of armour that was lurking in an alcove until he passed. When he was far enough away, Larker tiptoed down the hall. She passed a large wooden door with a sign that read:

MR BLACK'S ARTS

Larker's nosiness got the better of her, and she bent down to peer through the keyhole.

Inside was an art studio, presided over by a man with a shock of black hair, a black goatee beard and all-black clothes. He paced up and down the classroom, barking at the children.

"MR BLACK WANTS BLACK, BLACK AND **MORE** BLACK!"

However, from the look of things, you couldn't have more black. All the paint was black, and all the paper was black too. The pupils' pictures were nothing more than blocks of black.

This wasn't art. This was torture.

Larker shook her head in disbelief. The more you explored **THE CRUEL SCHOOL,** the crueller it became. You could say one good thing about the place – it lived up to its name.

Suddenly shadows flashed on the wall. There were two figures, one tall and upright, the other short and squat. The short one was pushing a large piece of heavy equipment on a trolley. It looked like a huge glass tank, like a display case in which you might keep a stuffed animal.

Just as Larker tried to follow, the shadows disappeared from view. The passages of the castle were like a maze, and it was impossible to know which way they went. Larker was seriously spooked, and tiptoed as quietly as she could. Not far off, she heard the sound of feet clattering on the floor. It sounded like a PE class. Larker was intrigued to discover exactly what games were played at **THE CRUEL SCHOOL**, so she took another few paces to reach the door.

The sign read:

DANGER! SPORTS HALL!

Indeed, the sport being played inside was DEADLY DANGEROUS. A round lady in a tracksuit was leading the children in a game of dodgeball.

But this was dodgeball with a difference.

There was no ball!

Instead, the teacher, Miss Ball, rolled herself up into a ball and then bowled herself at the children.

ROLL!

She was an expert at the roly-poly game and knocked over a crowd of children who were all cowering behind each other like skittles!

B A S H !
BISH!
BOSH!

They flew through the air…

"ARGH!"

"HELP!"

"STOP!"

…before landing in a heap
on the other side of the room.

THUD!

Suddenly there was the
deafening sound of rattling
crockery. Larker opened the nearest door, which
had a sign that read LOST PROPERTY OFFICE , and
hid inside. Peering through a crack in the door, she
spied Rank. The dinner lady was wheeling a trolley
piled high with all the broken bowls and plates from
breakfast time. She was cursing under her breath.

"If I ever see that wretched girl again, I
will scramble her and serve her up for
breakfast!"

Oops! thought Larker. She waited until
the coast was clear before slipping out of
the dark and smelly room.

The sign on the next door read:

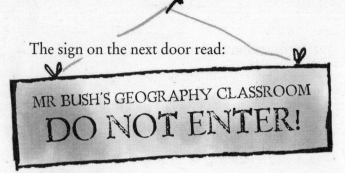

MR BUSH'S GEOGRAPHY CLASSROOM
DO NOT ENTER!

Looking through a little window near the top of
the door, Larker was surprised to see a ruddy-faced
teacher with a beard, in a fur coat, goggles and snow
boots, standing on top of a
huge mountain of ice
and snow.

All the children looked up at him from their desks, their faces painted with FEAR.

"Because of your atrocious behaviour," announced the teacher, Mr Bush, "the bad news is that the field trip to the North Pole has been cancelled!"

"OH!" moaned the kids in unison. Together they sounded like someone had stepped on a set of bagpipes.

"But the good news is that the North Pole is coming to you!"

Mr Bush began pushing the ice and snow with his boots.

CRUNCH!

Soon an AVALANCHE was sliding through the classroom...

WHOOSH!

...burying the children up to their armpits.

"NOOOOOOOOOO!" they cried.

"NO! IT'S NOT 'NOOOOOOOOOO'! IT'S SNOOOOOW! HO! HO! HO!" hooted Mr Bush.

Immediately, a snowball fight broke out.

WHOOSH!

SPLAT!

WHOOSH!

SPLAT!

WHOOSH!

SPLAT!

A stray snowball hit Larker square in the face!

SPLAT!

It gave her an ice beard!

"**SQUAWK!**" echoed around the school. This time the pelican was signalling the end of school. The classroom doors were flung open and children began swarming back to their rooms. To avoid being dragged to DETENTION by Gibber, Larker hurried further away from the throng. However, she was shocked to discover that THE CRUEL SCHOOL had a library.

Not just any old library.

No.

Spelled out in big, bold letters over the tall wooden doors were the words…

Chapter 15
THE LIBRARY OF DOOM

How can a library be full of doom? thought Larker. *How silly!*

Larker was someone who liked to make AN ENTRANCE. That way she would always be noticed. So she swung open the library doors dramatically...

WHOOSH!

...only to find herself completely ignored.

The elderly librarian was slumped at a dark wooden counter with a huge tin of biscuits. A sign on her desk read:

MISS DUNK
THE CRUEL SCHOOL LIBRARIAN

She was far too involved in dunking biscuits in her tea to notice Larker's entrance.

As she passed the librarian, Larker noticed that strange ticking sound again.

TICK TOCK TICK TOCK!

She scanned the walls for a clock, but there wasn't one. Then she took in the library, which must have been the messiest library in the world. It was a **riot** of books. Books were piled up on the floor, on chairs and tables. Books on shelves were stacked in such a haphazard way that they were either upside down or with the pages facing out.

At first, Larker was struck by the categories of books on offer. They all seemed to be horrible ones.

There were no joke books or funny books or books full of cute pictures of puppies or anything like that.

Instead, there were shelves and shelves of books that would give the children of **THE CRUEL SCHOOL** NIGHTMARES.

The titles themselves were appalling enough to have you fleeing the library in fear.

A SPOTTER'S GUIDE TO SPOTS

SOCKS THAT KILL

MISS GIBBER'S
GUIDE TO GABBER

EVERYTHING YOU EVER WANTED
TO KNOW ABOUT FOOT CHEESE*

*BUT WERE AFRAID TO ASK

MONSTERS THAT EAT CHILDREN
FOR BREAKFAST, LUNCH & DINNER

THE WORLD'S SMELLIEST BOTTOM BURPS
(A SCRATCH 'N' SNIFF BOOK)

MAGGOTS ON TOAST AND ONE HUNDRED
OTHER MOUTHWATERING RECIPES
BY MISS RANK

BEAUTIFUL PAINTINGS OF STEAMING COWPATS

**MR DIGITS'S EASY GUIDE
TO COUNTING TO TEN**

MYSTERIOUS DISAPPEARANCES
AT THE CRUEL SCHOOL

Larker began browsing the shelves, looking for a book, any book, that would **not** give her nightmares.

Needless to say, she couldn't find a thing.

Just then, the doors swung open and the littlest kid in the school hurried in.

Bug!

The boy was sweating profusely and looked gravely ill. He darted behind some shelves and installed himself there out of sight.

Larker peered round the shelves to see him slumped on a pile of books, his little legs not reaching the floor. Despite his small size, he was holding a weighty red leatherbound tome, which was nearly as tall as he was. In gold lettering was the title of the book:

The unusual thing was that Bug was holding the book the wrong way up, so the writing was upside down. He made sure the book covered his face so no one could see it was him.

"What are you doing in here?" asked Larker.

"Go away!" he hissed.

"No. I asked you a question!"

"I am meant to be in DETENTION again, but I'm hiding in here."

"Is it as bad as everyone says?"

"Yep! I had one yesterday too."

"What happened?"

"I don't remember it at all," he replied. Bug was still sweating profusely and loosened his collar to try to cool down.

"It was only yesterday!"

"I know, but I can't remember anything that happened other than walking through the door. Everything after that is a blur."

"That is weird."

"I had this nightmare last night that I was blazing through the sky on fire."

"That is weird too."

"What is also weird is that I have been feeling super-hot all day. Like I am burning up!" He fanned his face with the book.

"You don't look well. Shouldn't you be in the sick bay?"

The boy snorted. "No thanks! The sick bay at **THE CRUEL SCHOOL** is there to make you sick. I am going to hide out here. Now please just BOG OFF!"

"Why are libraries so tall? Because they have so many stories!"

"BOG OFF!"

"Why did the librarian fall down? She was in the non-friction section!"

"BOG. OFF."

"Where does the library keep books about Big Foot? The large print section!"

"For the last time, just BOG OFF!"

"All right! All right! Just trying to lighten the mood!" replied Larker before walking over to the far side of the library.

She loitered there for a while, leafing through a book on bogeys, before she heard a **SIZZLING** noise.

"Bug?" she called out, running over to see what was going on.

Bug had a look of deep distress on his face. It was a similar look to the one you have when you desperately need the loo but don't think you're going to get there in time.

"Are you all right, Bug?" asked Larker, knowing full well that the answer was "no".

But the boy couldn't speak. Instead, his face

glowed redder and redder and redder until it looked like a giant strawberry.

"What's going on, Bug?" she pressed. "Tell me! PLEASE!"

Still he couldn't answer, but there was a terrible look of dread in his eyes. It was as if he desperately wanted to tell her something, but just couldn't get it out.

As his face glowed as hot as the sun, he dropped the book he was holding.

DONK!

Larker's eyes flashed over to where the librarian was sitting. But Miss Dunk was too busy dunking to notice anything amiss.

MISS DUNK
THE CRUEL SCHOOL LIBRARIAN

Bug fell off the stack of books he was sitting on and began convulsing on the floor. Smoke was coming out of his ears. He looked as if he were going to…

EXPLODE!

Chapter 16
THE EXPLODING BOY

"**B**UG!" yelled Larker, trying to pull the boy to his feet.

Then the strangest thing in a long list of strange things happened. Flames started to fly out of Bug's behind.

FIZZLE! FAZZLE! FOZZLE!

"What's happening, Bug?" cried Larker as she held him up. She called over to the elderly librarian: "MISS DUNK! HELP!"

But Dunk didn't look up from her dunking.

Now the heat that was coming off the boy was like that of a furnace.

Then Bug's feet lifted off the ground.

He was taking off!

Larker reached out her hands and placed them on his shoulders to try to hold him down. But it was impossible.

"STOP!" she cried, the skin on her hands burning with the heat.

The flames grew and grew until…

K A B O O M !

…Bug shot through the air like a METEOR! He bounced off the walls…

BISH! BASH! BOSH!

…before he whizzed up to the ceiling…

CRASH!

…smashing through the roof of the library.

Larker took cover under a mighty encyclopedia of monsters, as debris fell to the floor.

C R U M B L E !

Looking up through the
cloud of dust, Larker spotted
a boy-sized hole in the roof.

Beyond that, Bug was
whizzing through the air,
heading straight for the clouds.

KABOOM!

An explosion lit up the sky in a deep red, before a
figure plummeted in the direction of the sea.

Larker rushed over to the librarian, who was still
trying and failing to dunk her biscuit into her cup
of tea.

"MISS DUNK!" shouted the girl.

With that, Dunk's dunked biscuit broke off and
fell into the tea.

"Look what you have made me do!"
exclaimed Dunk.

"Miss," spluttered Larker, "I thought you ought to know…"

"KNOW WHAT?"

" A small boy just exploded!"

PART TWO

THE SECRETS BELOW

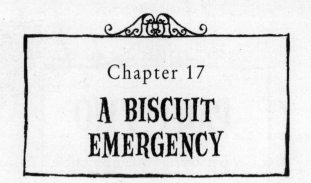

Chapter 17
A BISCUIT EMERGENCY

"A boy just exploded? You must have gone bananas!" spluttered the elderly librarian from behind the counter.

"NO! I am definitely not bananas or cuckoo in the coconut!" protested Larker.

"I have a good mind to report you to the headmistress!"

"I have a good mind to send YOU to the headmistress!" replied Larker.

"Well, you can't!"

"Why not?"

"It is strictly forbidden to disturb the professor! She is a very busy lady!"

"Busy doing what?" exclaimed Larker. "This school is an absolute disgrace."

"How dare you!"

"I do dare!"

"You've barely been here a day and you're already making trouble!"

"And I will carry on making trouble. Lots of trouble! NOW COME ON! FOLLOW ME! QUICK!" shouted Larker.

"I just need to finish my tea and biscuits!" replied Dunk.

"THERE ISN'T TIME!"

Larker heaved the old lady up out of her seat.

"OOH! I AM HALF DUNKED!" cried Dunk as the tea-soaked half of her gingernut biscuit splattered on the floor.

SPLUT!

Trying her best not to trip over the random piles of books, Larker hauled Dunk out of the library's tall double doors.

BOSH!

Then they all but tumbled down the steep stone staircase.

DONK! DONK! DONK!

Finally, they reached a patch of shrubland that doubled as a playing field for the school. Now there were just a few glowing embers floating through the air. They were snuffed out as they settled on the sea.

"Well, child!" huffed Dunk. "Where is this **exploding boy?**"

Larker replied, "He exploded, miss. So he's... well, not here any more."

"Perhaps you just heard the volcano rumbling!"

"No! It wasn't that. It was an **exploding boy!**"

"An **exploding boy** indeed! What utter balderdash!"

"If it is balderdash, why is there a great big hole in the roof of the library?"

"Is there?"

"**Yes!** Come on!" exclaimed Larker. She grabbed the librarian by the hand and dragged her back up the stone steps.

"Not again!" complained Dunk.

But when they returned to the library, the strangest thing had happened. Right where Bug had been sitting, there was now a **huge** rock.

"This wasn't here before!" protested Larker.

"What the blazes is that doing in my library?" barked Dunk. "I need another biscuit! In fact, I need two biscuits! And fast! This is a biscuit emergency!"

Just then, a birdlike figure fluttered in from behind one of the bookshelves. Her black gown swept behind her like wings.

~ F L U T T E R !

"Well, I never! If I am not mistaken, this is a meteor!"

she announced.

The sound of her voice sent a shiver down Larker's back. It was like the hiss of a snake.

"Ooh, Doctor Doktur!" cooed Dunk.

"I didn't see you

hiding there!"

Chapter 18
DOCTOR DOKTUR

"I just stepped out of my laboratory for a moment to see what all the hullabaloo was about," purred Doctor Doktur. The Science teacher was tall and elegant, with a shock of white like a lightning bolt going through the middle of her black hair.

"Is your name Doctor Doctor?" asked Larker.

"No!" she stated firmly. "Being named Doctor Doctor would be ridiculous. My name is Doctor Doktur."

"That's what I just said!" replied Larker. "Doctor Doctor!"

"DOCTOR DOKTUR!"

"DOCTOR DOCTOR?"

"DOCTOR DOKTUR!"

Larker was mightily confused. "It doesn't sound any different to me!"

The Science teacher's red eyes narrowed as the librarian looked on, concerned that the mood was taking a dark turn. "I am a doctor, and my surname is Doktur. D. O. K. T. U. R. So I am Doctor Doktur. Doktur is completely different from doctor!"

"Well, it's spelled differently!" scoffed Larker.

"And *Doktur* sounds completely different from *doctor*."

"A tiny bit different! Hey, Doctor, Doctor!" began the girl. She just couldn't help herself. As a lover of silly jokes, someone with a funny name was comedy gold! "I feel like a pair of curtains! Well, pull yourself together! Doctor, Doctor! I've swallowed my pocket money! Take this and we'll see if there's any change in the morning! Doctor, Doctor! I think I need glasses! You certainly do – this is the fish-and-chip shop!"

"Ha! Ha!" chuckled Dunk. "I hadn't heard that last one!"

"So answer me this, Doctor Doktur," said Larker as she skipped around her. "Why did you put this meteor here?"

Doctor Doktur's red eyes narrowed.

"I didn't," she answered calmly, as if she were well practised at lying. "It must have just landed here. Hence the hole!"

"No!" snapped Larker, losing her cool. "Bug was sitting right there. He took off and zoomed through the roof!"

Now it was the doctor's turn to laugh. It was mocking laughter. She looked over at Dunk who dutifully joined in.

"HA! HA! HA!"

"That must be why you were sent here to THE CRUEL SCHOOL," purred Doctor Doktur. "For lying!"

Larker felt rage rising up from her toes, but before it came out of her mouth in a torrent of angry words she just managed to stop herself.

"No," she replied calmly. "I am not a liar. I was sent here for putting a whoopee cushion on the headmistress's chair, but I didn't do it!"

"Of course you didn't!" chirped the teacher. "What a loathsome little liar!"

"I am not a liar! My parents taught me right from wrong!"

"Oh! Did they really? And where are they now?"

"Gone," said the orphan with sorrow in her eyes.

"If they were here now, they would be ashamed of you. Just look at you. You are the perfect picture of guilt! Miss Dunk! I suggest you call for Meddle to have this hole in the roof repaired. In the meantime, if you will excuse me, I must return to my DETENTION."

With that, the teacher did a little curtsy and waltzed towards the door.

Larker summoned up all her courage to shout after her,

"STOP RIGHT THERE!"

Chapter 19
DUNKING DISASTER!

The shock of being shouted at did indeed stop the teacher in her tracks. Doctor Doktur was a lady who oozed malevolence. No one **ever** shouted at her. Her red eyes widened in disbelief, before a sinister smile crept across her face.

"I do believe the new girl," began Doktur, "is already barking orders at the teachers!"

"I didn't want to be rude, but..." spluttered Larker.

"Oh! She didn't want to be rude! Did you hear that, Miss Dunk?"

The librarian looked up from her tea. "I'm so sorry – I wasn't listening. I was too busy doing a devilishly difficult double dunk!"

True to her word, Dunk did indeed have not one but two chocolate fingers in her fingers: two chocolate fingers that she was dunking together like synchronised swimmers into her now distinctly chocolatey tea.

MISS DUNK
THE CRUEL SCHOOL LIBRARIAN

Dunk dunked the chocolate fingers in her tea for too long and they melted.

PLOP! PLOP!

"NOOOOOOOOO!" wailed Dunk. "IT IS A DUNKING DISASTER!"

"I saw what I saw, Doctor... er... Doktur!" protested Larker.

"But Bug couldn't have **zoomed** up through the air!"

"Why not?"

"Because right now he is in my Science laboratory taking DETENTION."

Larker was speechless for a moment before uttering, "But that's impossible!"

"It's not impossible. It's true.

Please, child, come and see

for yourself!"

Chapter 20
A WONDERLAND OF WEIRDNESS

After hurrying along the maze of hallways, Doktur and Larker reached the Science laboratory.

The teacher swung open the door and performed a little bow of her head. **"Please. After you!"** She gestured towards her enormous classroom, letting Larker step inside first.

A bulky man in a too-small lab coat and thick red rubber gloves was standing in front of a boy with his back to Larker.

The man smiled sinisterly, revealing all silver teeth. He had a shiny bald head, not that you could see it because squatting right there on top acting as a wig was a cat —

a real live cat named Fiend. The cat may have only had one eye and one leg, but she still made a wildly unconvincing wig. However, a cat is not the absolute **worst** animal you could choose to disguise your baldness:

A **squirrel's** bushy tail would make it a dead giveaway.

N I B B L E !

N I B B L E !

← A **tarantula**

would weave a web over your face and, before you knew it, you would not be able to see a thing.

S P I N !

A **rabbit** spends all its time munching carrots. No one wants a head of hair that chomps.

MUNCH!

Owls would scratch your head with their sharp talons.

S C R I T C H !
S C R A T C H !
S C R O T C H !

A small **bear**, even a baby one, is far too heavy.

DOOF!

Monkeys just can't sit still. They would leap around on their bottoms.

BOING! BOING! BOING!

An **otter** is way too slippery and would slide straight off.

SLIP!

A **sheep** would make far too much noise.

"BAAAH!"

154

A penguin might lay
an egg on your head.

PLOP!

 Foxes pong. And they hate shampoo.
And conditioner.

PONG!

Grunt had on a pair of very strange
round glasses. They weren't the kind you
could see through. Instead, there was a **spiral**
on each lens, which was spinning. The effect was
hypnotising.

"Take those off, Grunt!" snapped Doktur.

Grunt swiped off the glasses and hid them in his
laboratory coat pocket. The one-legged cat woke up
and hissed.

"HISS!"

Looking at Doktur and Grunt, Larker realised

they were the figures whose shadows she'd seen in the hallway just before the end of school.

"What are those glasses for?" she asked.

"Just silly spectacles to amuse the kiddywinkies!" replied Doktur.

"I asked *him*!" said Larker.

Doktur's expression soured. "I am afraid my laboratory assistant, Grunt, is a man of few words. Indeed, no words."

"He doesn't speak at all?" asked Larker.

"Oh no. He communicates only in grunts. Don't you, Grunt?"

Grunt grunted in reply. "**HURR!**"

"What did that mean?" asked Larker.

"Yes!" replied Doktur. "One grunt for yes, two grunts for no."

"**HURR!**" grunted Grunt in agreement.

Larker scoured the Science laboratory. It was a wonderland of weirdness. The classroom was dominated by a huge stained-glass window, like those you might see in a church. Except this stained-glass window depicted Doctor Doktur herself! The Science teacher was shown smiling sinisterly with bits and bobs of science equipment floating around her.

She's so full of herself! thought Larker, though she didn't dare say it.

As you might expect from a laboratory, there were chemical charts and diagrams on the walls, racks of test tubes on shelves and jumbles of metal boxes with wires poking out scattered everywhere. Jars with all sorts of strange pickled creatures in them were gathering dust:

A three-winged pelican

A nine-legged octopus

A two-tailed baby shark

Plus, there were stuffed animals arranged in enormous glass tanks:

A flock of dodos

A sabre-toothed tiger

A vulture in flight

A black rhinoceros

A giant bat

A howling wolf on two legs, which looked more like a werewolf

A woolly mammoth

A crocodile with one large eye in the middle of its head like a cyclops

A white-haired gorilla with dazzling scarlet eyes

Conjoined twin polar bears with two roaring heads

Curiously, there were also clockwork toys that looked as if they'd been handmade: life-sized clockwork robots of an owl, a rabbit and a tortoise. Next to them was a wax head of Doctor Doktur herself, which looked hauntingly real.

On a huge shelf above, there was a chunk of moon rock, a cooled-down lump of what once was molten lava, presumably from the volcano, and next to it a wide empty space where only dust remained. Larker's mind began whirring. Was this where the meteor had come from?

On a higher shelf crouched a huge machine with

a thick set of wires spun round in a coil.

"What's that?" asked Larker, pointing to it.

"Oh! You haven't been concentrating in Science class, have you?" purred Doktur. "We will have to arrange extra lessons. That is an electromagnet."

"What's it for?"

"Let me show you. Grunt, you don't mind, do you?"

"HURR! HURR!" replied Grunt, which meant no.

"Splendid!" announced Doktur. "Grunt has metal teeth because he ate too many sweets. And when I flick this switch..."

Grunt grabbed on to the nearest counter, and the cat dug her claws into his head. They knew what was coming.

Doktur flicked the switch on the electromagnet. The machine hummed and Grunt took off, flying head first across the laboratory.

WHOOSH!

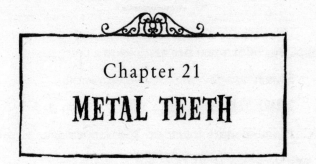

Chapter 21
METAL TEETH

Grunt's metal teeth stuck to the electromagnet.

CLANK!

"HURR! HURR!" he grunted.

"The world's most powerful electromagnet!" said Doktur proudly and switched it off.

Grunt immediately fell to the floor of the laboratory.

DOOF!

"HURR! HURR!" he grunted.

"Thank you so much for agreeing to take part in that experiment, Grunt!"

"HURR! HURR!"

"HISS!" hissed the cat.

Larker ran over to Grunt.

"Are you all right?" she asked, trying to help him

up. But he slapped her hand away.

SLAP!

"HURR! HURR!"

Now at the front of the laboratory, Larker spotted a boy in DETENTION.

SPOD!

Her friend was sitting motionless on a stool, his face devoid of expression.

"Spod! SPOD! It's Larker!" she said, but he didn't react in any way. "What has happened to you?"

Spod said nothing. He didn't even blink. Had those strange **spiral** glasses Grunt had been wearing **zomb-☺-fied** him? Larker turned to Doktur.

"What have you done to Spod? And where's Bug?" she demanded. "You told me he was here!"

The teacher chuckled to herself. "Ha! Ha!"

"I don't see what's so funny!" said Larker.

"What's funny is that Bug is right here, isn't he, Grunt?"

"**HURR!**" grunted Grunt.

"I know he is short, which might be why he is so difficult to spot," said Doktur. "Grunt, would you be so kind, please?"

The laboratory technician waddled over to the front of the class. He reached down and picked up a little boy by his nose. He dangled there, only the back of his head visible, but soon Grunt spun him round, and Larker gasped in shock when she saw

it was indeed...

BUG!

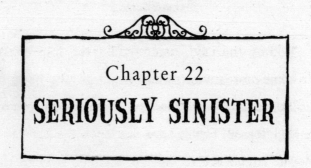

Chapter 22
SERIOUSLY SINISTER

How could Bug have just exploded in the sky and yet five minutes later be here in DETENTION?

There was something seriously sinister going on at this school.

Grunt dangled the little boy by his nose, his expression changing to one that almost resembled a smile, flashing his metal teeth.

"Bug!" began Doktur. "The new girl here thought you had exploded! Isn't that funny?"

"HURR! HURR! HURR!" grunted Grunt in a pantomime of laughter.

"Grunt?" asked Doktur.

"HURR?"

"Please ensure this young lady gets back to her room safely."

"I know the way!" protested Larker, desperate to do some more investigating.

"No, no, no," purred Doktur. "I insist. You are new here, after all. Grunt, have you seen the caretaker Meddle anywhere?"

"**HURR!**" Grunt grunted.

"Please ask him to check Miss er..."

"Larker. Everyone calls me Larker."

"Very apt. Do ask Meddle to check Miss Larker stays in her room tonight. We would hate for her to come to any harm," she purred, an evil glint in her eye.

"**HURR!**" grunted Grunt, and he let go of Bug's nose. The boy slumped to the ground.

DOOF!

SIZZLE!

Larker noticed something super strange. The boy was wet through but sizzling like a sausage.

"BUG?" said the girl. "Are you all right?" She reached out to him.

"Don't touch him!" barked Doktur.

"Why not?" demanded Larker.

"This wretched boy is riddled with fleas! That is why he is so hot. He can't stop scratching himself!"

Larker made a dash for Bug.

"GRUNT! SEIZE HER!" barked Doktur.

"HURR!" grunted Grunt, pacing towards the girl.

Larker was terrified. She backed away from the brute and cowered behind one of the stools. Using his big hands, which were more like paws, the laboratory technician whacked the stool out of the way.

THWUCK!

It flew across the room, narrowly missing the top of Spod's head, before smashing into pieces against the wall.

B O O M !

Then Grunt picked up the girl by both ears.

"I am perfectly happy to walk!" said Larker as she was carted out of the room.

STOMP!
STOMP!
STOMP!

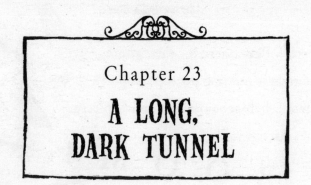

Chapter 23
A LONG, DARK TUNNEL

In a few painful moments, Larker found herself back in her cramped room. Meddle made sure she was not going anywhere as…

CLUNK!

…he locked her in.

"Sweet dreams, Your Royal Highness!" he said as he and Grunt made their way back along the hallway, chuckling to themselves. Even Fiend, the one-eyed, one-legged cat on Grunt's head, allowed herself an evil little laugh.

"HISS! HISS! HISS!"

Fiend was without doubt the evillest cat in the world. Other notable malevolent moggies include:

Podge, a cat who ate a small

dog for breakfast, lunch and dinner. And a big dog for Sunday lunch with all the trimmings...

Bandit, a cat who stole so much money from its owners that it had its own cat house built that was much bigger than theirs...

Gnaw, a cat who took great delight in chewing the toes of its owner.

Boo, a cat who bared its fangs and hissed at old ladies who tried to stroke it. The poor souls would run a mile...

Spoil, a cat who would rip all the furniture to shreds with its claws as soon as its owners left the house and blame it on the puppy...

Sozzle, a cat who demanded champagne instead of milk in its bowl…

Blot, a cat who loved ruining children's parties by scoffing all the jelly and ice cream, ripping open the Pass the Parcel parcel and popping all the balloons with its claws…

Spit, a cat who took great pleasure in coughing up furballs on to your dinner plate…

Larker clutched her boiling hot ears, still ringing from the pain of being carried by them. Down but not out, she was more determined than ever to discover what was really going on at THE CRUEL SCHOOL. She climbed up to look through the tiny window. From there, she could just see the roof of the library. It was getting dark, but she could spot

the broken tiles scattered around the hole in the roof. If that meteor really had crashed through the roof from above, then the tiles would have fallen inwards, not outwards.

The night was the best time to investigate further. So Larker waited until it was completely dark before going to work.

The floor of Larker's room was a jumble of huge stone slabs, each one weighing as much as a really fat cat – one of those humongous ones you can barely pick up. (And if you do pick it up, then you have to immediately put it down again for fear of dropping it. Ones that have to be ferried around in a wheelbarrow. You know the type.)

Along the sides of these stone slabs were grooves into which little fingers could just poke. Larker had noticed that one of the stone slabs in the corner of her room creaked a little when she stood on it. When she ran her fingers along its side, she saw that someone had rubbed some of the dirt away. Digging the tips of her fingers under the slab, she found that it was loose. She lifted up the slab and placed it gently on the ground.

On the underside of the slab, someone had chalked the words:

BEWARE THE INVISIBLE DOOR!

They must have been scrawled by a previous occupant of Larker's room. Peering down, she saw a long, dark tunnel stretching out below her. She had no idea where it led, but she was just small enough to squeeze through the hole. She jumped down, pulling the slab back into place as she did so.

The tunnel was rough and uneven and must have been dug by hand. It ended above the ceiling of the toilets. They were even more **stinktastic*** than she could ever have imagined, positively medieval.

---

* *A real word you will find in your* Walliamsictionary, *the greatest reference book of made-up words in the known universe.*

STINKOMETER

RUNNY CHEESE

SWEATY SOCKS

ROTTEN CABBAGE

USED TISSUES

A BUCKET OF RABBIT DROPPINGS

HUNDRED-YEAR-OLD YOGHURT

A HIPPOPOTAMUS'S BURP

A HIPPOPOTAMUS'S BOTTOM FART

THE CRUEL SCHOOL TOILETS

Larker lifted one of the wooden ceiling panels and slid down through the gap. Balancing precariously on one of the damp toilet seats, she pulled the panel back into place. As she did so, her foot slipped off the seat, and she ended up plunging into the bowl.

SPLOSH!

Larker winced as she felt the wetness cling to her. Goodness knows what was in here. She was sure **THE CRUEL SCHOOL** kids never flushed the toilet. In fact, when she reached for the chain to pull herself back up, she realised it wasn't even there! Larker yanked her foot out of the U-bend and scuttled over to the toilet door, leaving a trail of bog water in her wake.

SPLAT! SPLAT! SPLAT!

The door opened on to the castle's central courtyard. Immediately, Larker could feel the spray of saltwater from the sea on her face. Her destination was the Library of Doom. She wanted to investigate the damage to the roof further. If she could prove the hole wasn't made by a meteor, then this would point the finger of suspicion at Doctor Doktur.

Larker kept close to the stone walls to stay out of sight. It was deadly dark now, but the castle was illuminated by a haunting low moon.

She tiptoed over to a drainpipe on the wall of the library. She put her hands on it. It was wet and slippery, but she just managed to heave herself up.

Then, she felt something or someone looming behind her. A hand came down on her shoulder. Frozen in fear, Larker opened her mouth but couldn't let out a scream...

Chapter 24
WORMS

"SHUSH!" hissed the voice in her ear.

Slowly the girl turned round to see a face smiling back at her.

"Who are you?" she whispered, taking in this grubby little man. His thick, black, wiry hair and beard were dotted with grass, twigs and dead leaves. They were **rustling** in the howling wind as the pair stood outside in the dark, with the sound of waves crashing against the rocks beneath them.

WOOMPH!

"Worms!" replied the man.

"Worms?" exclaimed the girl.

"It's me nickname. I'm the gardener here. I always have worms in me pockets, so I think that's why they call me that," he said. Worms had a lovely country burr to his voice, which immediately set the girl at ease.

"I'm Larker. So, Worms, have you got any worms on you now?" she asked.

"Just the one – **Wormy!**" chirped Worms.

"Great name!" remarked the girl sarcastically. "It must have taken you ages to come up with that!"

Worms produced a wriggly little worm from his

coat pocket and dangled it in front of her nose.

"Beautiful, isn't she?"

"'Beautiful' is not the first word I would use when describing a worm!"

"Don't be like that! You'll hurt her feelings!" said Worms. The gardener gave his pet worm a kiss on the nose (well, I hope it was her nose – it's hard to tell with a worm which end is which) and put her safely back in his pocket.

"How can you tell which end of a worm is which? Tickle it in the middle to see which end laughs!" said Larker.

"HA! HA!" laughed Worms.

"What reads and lives in an apple? A bookworm!"

"HA! HA!"

"Why are glow-worms good to carry in your bag? They can lighten your load!"

"HA! HA!"

"I can't believe you like my jokes!"

"Oh! I love a good joke. Even a good bad one like that!"

"Oh!" replied Larker, a little miffed.

"No one cracks jokes here on the island. And I've been stuck in this place for fifty years."

"Good grief!"

"I started off here as a pupil."

"Is that so?"

"Then when I'd done my time the headmistress made me the gardener. I had nowhere else to go. But right now you've got some explaining to do…"

"Me?" replied Larker, trying to appear as innocent as possible.

"Yes, you! I was just sitting there in me shed," he said, pointing to the little wooden hut on the edge of the cliff. "Me and Wormy were just sharing me mug of tea, and I saw a spooky figure moving about in the darkness. I know all the children are meant to be in bed by now. So what are you doing out of your room, miss?"

"Well… I was just… er, going to, you know," she spluttered, "see if I could repair the hole in the roof of the library."

"The one the boy blasted through?" replied Worms.

"You saw what I saw?" asked Larker, breathless with excitement.

"I saw the whole thing! He flew through the air like a..."

"METEOR!" they both said at once.

"SNAP!" exclaimed Larker. "So I haven't gone bananas!"

"No, unless we've both gone bananas," said Worms with a chuckle.

"I was in the library at the time. I saw everything. It was this boy called Bug, the littlest in the school."

"Was it now?"

"Fire shot right out of his bottom."

"Sounds painful."

"Then he *zoomed* up into the air and **exploded**," explained Larker.

Worms nodded. "I saw the flames light up the sky."

"So how come Bug was in DETENTION five minutes later?"

"Was he now?" asked Worms. Then the gardener looked lost in thought. "Maybe that's why I saw Grunt ordering the boatman to take him out to sea...?"

"So that's where Bug landed?"

"Must have. I rushed out of the shed to try to get a better view, but you know the caretaker?"

"Sadly, yes."

"Meddle spied me having a snoop and ordered me back in me shed!"

"So, he's in on it too?" asked Larker.

"In on what?"

"I don't know. Yet."

"All I know is that there's peculiar goings-on going on at this school," he whispered.

Larker gulped. There was terror in the man's eyes.

"What do you mean?" pressed Larker.

"I've said too much," replied Worms.

"No! You haven't said enough!"

"You need to get to bed!"

"No! I don't!" declared Larker. "I need to be up all night doing detective work! I want to find out what that Doctor Doktur is up to!"

"Keep your voice down!" hissed Worms. "If they spot you here, it won't just be you in deep doo-doo. It will be me in the deep doo-doo too!"

"Then tell me what you know…"

Worms squirmed. "Oh no."

"Oh yes!" replied Larker, loud enough to make Worms wince.

"It's too dangerous," he pleaded.

"I love danger!"

"You might see things that are horrifying!"

"I love being horrified!"

Worms smiled. "Well then, follow me, if you dare…"

"I do dare! I do! In fact, why don't you follow me?" asked Larker, stepping on her tippy-toes to feel taller.

The gardener shook his head and said, "Because you don't know where we're going!"

"Oh yes!" she replied. "Go on, then! Lead the way!"

The next thing Larker knew, Worms was leading her down some
stone steps
into the
darkest depths
of the
castle...

Chapter 25
THE INVISIBLE DOOR

Larker wasn't easily spooked, but there were all manner of horrors in the vaults of the school: bats, rats, spiders as big as your hand…

It was dark down there. Larker walked straight into a spider's web, which entangled her.

"EURGH!" she cried as she felt a big, furry beast crawl on to her head.

Worms picked the giant spider off her and said, "Don't be scared, my little darling," to the spider!

Larker huffed loudly and demanded, "What are we even doing down here?"

"During the nights, I've seen some strange comings and goings in these here vaults."

"Who was coming and who was going?" she asked.

"I saw that Science teacher, Doctor Doctor Doktur—"

"It's just two 'Doctors'!"

"Doctor Doktur and her assistant, Grunt, were coming AND going. They were coming with this big potato sack over his shoulder, and they were going without it…"

"What was in that sack?"

"I don't know. But it was big enough to carry a…"

"Child?" she asked.

The thought was so awful that Worms couldn't utter another word. Instead, he nodded his head.

"We need to find out what they are doing down here."

The pair passed through a series of cellars, each one darker and danker than the last. There was all sorts of junk down here: battered suits of armour, old oil paintings, bronze busts, rugs, even a rusty old cannon from THE CRUEL SCHOOL'S days as a castle. There was more recent junk too: classroom

chairs with only three legs, a battered hobby horse and a trampoline with a child-sized hole in it.

"I don't think there's anybody down here," hissed Larker.

"Shush!" shushed Worms. "I hear footsteps!"

Echoing down the vaults was indeed the sound of footsteps. It was definitely more than one person, probably two.

"Stay dead still!" whispered Worms. "Wormy! Stop wiggling!" he hissed to the worm in his pocket.

As Worms and Larker stayed still as statues, they spotted the shadows of two figures pass on the walls. It was Doctor Doktur and Grunt, and Grunt had a large potato sack over his shoulder. But what or who was in the sack?

As quickly as they had appeared, they disappeared from view. The sound of footsteps ceased. Ahead was a large stone wall without a door in sight. That was where Doktur and Grunt had been heading.

"It's like they vanished into air!" said Larker.

"Into thin air!"

"There's no way back up to the ground if you come this way. Only the flight of steps we came down at the far end."

"BEWARE THE INVISIBLE DOOR!" recited the girl. "It was a message scratched on the bottom of a stone in my room!"

"Invisible door? I've been at this school for fifty years, and I don't know diddly-squat about no **invisible door!**"

"Maybe because it is invisible!"

"You have got a point there. But if it said

'BEWARE THE INVISIBLE DOOR' let's beware it, then!"

"Boring!" replied Larker. "Let's see if we can find it!"

She began tracing her hands along the wall, searching for anything that felt odd. Meanwhile, Worms gave the girl a strange look. A strange look that said *you are strange*. But that look changed as soon as her little fingers found a loose stone.

"Look!" she said, moving the stone around. "It wiggles!"

"So does my worm. So what?"

"So it could be something."

The girl wiggled the stone this way and that, up and down, all around. She was just about to give up when...

CLUNK!

Like a handle, the stone opened an invisible door in the wall.

"Oh! This invisible door?" lied Worms. "Of course I knew about this invisible door!"

"Liar! Liar! Pants on fire!"

The door was perfectly flush with the stone wall, so when closed it was indeed invisible. Beyond the door, it was as black as night.

"Well, you found the invisible door – well done. Now, I think it's time we both got some sleep," said Worms.

Larker shook her head. "Sleep is for squares! Come on!"

With that,

she

stepped

into

the

darkness.

Chapter 26
THE SECRET CAVE

Larker realised she was standing at the top of a spiral staircase that coiled down into a vast cave. A long way below her, she could see figures moving in the gloom. They were illuminated only by flaming torches on the cave walls.

Larker beckoned for Worms to join her, and together they began tiptoeing down the long metal staircase. As they did so, the scene below slowly came into focus. It looked like an operating theatre had been set up deep down in the cave.

Half a dozen glass tanks were
arranged in a semicircle. They were
just like the ones housing all
the weird and wonderful
creatures in the Science
laboratory. All the
tanks were empty,
except one.

Bug was in it. Well, it *looked* like Bug, but he was glowing red and yellow like a meteor. He'd been turned into a MONSTER! The creature was banging on the glass. It looked like he was trying to escape, but the glass was so thick, it was impossible.

THUMP! THUMP! THUMP!

In the centre of the cave sat a huge metal table, which looked like it belonged in Rank's kitchen. Across the centre of the table was a thick leather strap. A mess of coloured wires snaked from the table to a huge machine.

The machine appeared home-made. There were parts of a record player, a cinema projector, even a lawnmower. Bits of it were wrapped in tinfoil, others held together by rubber bands.

Dangling high above the table by a chunky metal chain was something Worms recognised.

"So that's where my greenhouse went!" he remarked.

"Shush!" shushed Larker. "They'll hear us!"

From their hiding place halfway down the

staircase, Larker and Worms spied Doktur and Grunt busying themselves around the cave. Grunt still had the potato sack over his shoulder but emptied it out on to the metal table.

FLOP!

It was only when the bag was whisked away that Larker could see what, or rather *who*, it was.

"Spod!" she hissed.

The boy lay motionless on the table.

"SHUSH! They'll hear us!" whispered Worms.

"Oh! Please don't tell me he's gone!" spluttered Larker.

Worms leaned over to get a closer look. "No. He's still alive. Look, he's breathing."

Spod's chest was moving up and down. The boy *was* alive!

"Why have they brought Spod down here?" she asked.

"I don't know," replied Worms. "But I think we're about to find out."

"Follow me," said Larker, tiptoeing down to the bottom of the stairs. Worms shook his head, but reluctantly followed her. There was a counter nearby, which was home to a complex experiment. Test tubes and beakers full of brightly coloured liquids hummed away over the flames of Bunsen burners. The pair crouched down behind them, spying through the bubbling potions.

"What are they going to do to Spod?" whispered Larker. "Some kind of operation?"

"I don't know!" replied Worms.

"He told me once that if you get sent to one of Doctor Doktur's DETENTIONS you are never the same again. Look at poor Bug."

"It's monstrous."

Grunt fixed Spod down to the metal table with the leather strap. Next, he scurried off to the chunky metal chain and began lowering the greenhouse over the boy.

"NOT SO FAST!" chided Doktur.

Grunt slowed the pace, and the greenhouse clanked on the ground.

CLANK!

"Is the seal in place?" barked the teacher.

Grunt ran his sausage fingers along the bottom of the greenhouse before nodding to his mistress.

"Good work, Grunt," she said. "Now for the FORCE FIELD."

Doktur pulled on a lever and…

WHIZZ!

What looked like lightning danced all around the outside of the greenhouse. If it hadn't been so deadly, it would've been beautiful.

Then Doktur paced over to the machine.

"AH! My **MOnsterficatiOn MaChine!**" she cooed, hugging it for a moment.

"What's a **MOnsterficatiOn MaChine?**" asked Worms.

"It must be a machine that turns people into monsters," guessed Larker.

Doktur put on some goggles and thick black rubber gloves and opened a hatch on the machine. With tongs, she lifted out something red and hot and seemingly alive!

"What's she got there?" hissed Worms from behind the counter.

"It looks like…" began Larker, "a chunk of the meteor!"

"There's a huge one in Doktur's laboratory."

"I knew it! That must have been for the last experiment, with Bug! They turned him into a meteor!"

"This school is never going to do well with the inspectors," muttered the gardener.

Just then the teacher stood absolutely still and listened. "Did you hear something, Grunt? I swear I just heard voices."

Larker and Worms stayed still as statues. Was the game up?

"Listen!" whispered Doktur. "Is there someone else in my cave?"

"**HURR! HURR!**" grunted Grunt, which meant "no".

"How about you, Fiend? Did you hear something?"

The cat that crouched on top of the laboratory assistant's head opened her one good eye and sniffed the air.

S N I F F ! S N I F F !

Larker and Worms didn't dare breathe.

Fiend shook her head.

"It must have been an echo," purred Doktur. "Well, Grunt, we had many false starts with our experiments, but we got there in the end. Bug is our very first monster! **METEOR MAN!** But what do we have in store for young Spod?"

She paced over to a nearby cabinet, which bore the sign:

• CABINET OF CURIOSITIES •

This was a tall piece of wooden furniture with what looked like a hundred little drawers in it. Each one was labelled, but from far away where Larker and Worms were hiding they didn't have a hope of reading them.

"**Now where is 'S'?**" Doktur asked herself. Her beady eyes scrolled down all the little drawers until she found what she was looking for. Next, she took out a jar, which had something slippery and slimy shuffling inside it. It was as big as Grunt's thumb.

"Oh no!" hissed Larker. "She's going to turn Spod into a... slug!"

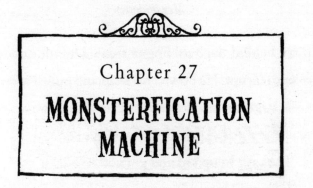

Chapter 27
MONSTERFICATION MACHINE

Clutching her metal tongs in her gloved hands, Doctor Doktur reached inside the jar. She plucked out the black slug, smirked to herself, then

placed it in the **MOnsterfication MaChine**. Hastily, she shut the door to stop the creepy-crawly from creepily crawling out.

As Larker and Worms spied from their hiding

place behind the bubbling potions, Doktur nodded over to Grunt. He bowed his head and pulled a lever.

A large circular stone in the floor slid away.

THONK!

The cave lit up red and gold.

"Oh no!" hissed Worms.

"What?" whispered Larker.

"The volcano! It's not dead! It's very much alive!"

Molten lava bubbled up from the hole in the cave.

"That means?" hissed Larker.

"It could go off at any time!"

Grunt picked up a metal pipe that was connected to the MOnsterfication MaChine and placed it in the lava.

"Now we have our lava power!" announced Doktur. "Let the MOnsterfication begin!"

She pressed a big red button and the MOnsterfication MaChine buzzed to life. There was whirring, bleeping and a loud whooshing noise.

W H I R R !

BLEEP! BLEEP!

W H O O O O O O S H !

All of a sudden, Spod's body pulsated with the energy flowing through him.

"We have to stop them!" shouted Larker.

The **MOnsterficatiOn MaChine** was so noisy that, even though she shouted, only Worms could hear her.

"It's too late!" he replied.

"NO! I HAVE TO SAVE SPOD!"

Larker jumped up from her hiding place, only to be yanked down by Worms.

"If they find you here, just think what they will do to you!" he said.

"But I have to help him!"

"I won't let you!" said Worms, holding on to her tightly. "It is too dangerous!"

Larker fell silent. She scrunched up her eyes, unable to watch her friend suffering for one second longer. Doktur spun the dial on the **MOnsterficatiOn MaChine**.

A LITTLE TOO MUCH DANGER!

A LOT TOO MUCH DANGER!

REALLY STOP NOW AS WE ARE VERY NEAR DANGER!

A FAIR AMOUNT OF DANGER!

A TINY BIT MORE DANGER!

A LITTLE BIT OF DANGER!

DANGER!

NO DANGER!

DANGER! DANGER!

DANGER! DANGER! DANGER!

For a moment, it felt as if the entire cave was going to fall in on itself, such was the commotion coming from the **MOnsterfication Machine**.

And then…

KABOOM!

There was a huge explosion.

Sparks flew everywhere.

FIZZ!

The flaming torches were blown out.

The circular stone over the lava slid back into place.

THONK!

ALL WAS SILENT. ALL WAS BLACK.

"A candle, Grunt!" came a cry in the darkness. It was Doktur. "A candle!"

"HURR!" came the reply.

There was the sound of footsteps before she shouted again, "A LIT candle, for goodness' sake!"

The sound of a match being struck fizzled through the gloom. The candle was lit, and now Doktur could examine her latest creation. She brought the flame close to the boy.

I say "boy", but Spod wasn't a boy any more.

He was some kind of monster.

A

SLUG

MONSTER!

Chapter 28
SLUG MONSTER

The monster was half boy and half slug. He had the face of a boy but the body of a slug.

"SLUG MONSTER! My greatest creation yet!" declared Doctor Doktur. **"Even greater than METEOR MAN!"**

"HURR!" grunted Grunt, grinning ghoulishly.

The beast writhed on the metal table, letting out a gruesome gurgle.

"GUG-GUG-GUG-GUG!"

Spod wasn't there any more. In his place was a creature guaranteed to give you nightmares.

From her hiding place behind the potions, Larker couldn't help herself. "NOOOO!" she cried at the horrifying sight.

"Shush!" shushed Worms.

But it was too late. The evil pair was on to them. Doktur's eyes lit up with wicked glee.

"Grunt!" she announced. "Up! Up! Up!"

"HURR!"

The wordless assistant knew what to do. He nodded and yanked the metal chain so the greenhouse went back up to the ceiling.

CLANK!

"Unleash the **SLUG MONSTER!**"

"HURR!"

The man untied the leather strap that held the beast in place. The monster slithered off the table on to the floor of the cave.

"**SLUG MONSTER! Find the** intruders!" ordered Doktur.

"NOW!"

SLUG MONSTER understood perfectly and began snaking around the cave. As he did, he left a silver trail of slime behind.

Larker and Worms stayed dead still and dead silent as the monster edged closer and closer. They were crouched on the other side of the counter, but the monster was sniffing them out with his tentacles. Finally, he opened his mouth wide to take a bite.

"ARGH!" screamed Larker. She pushed on the counter with all her might and Worms followed her lead. The counter toppled over, taking all the test tubes and beakers of bubbling potions with it.

SHUNT!

CRASH!

SMASH!

"GURGLE!" cried the creature, retreating.

"Who is there?" thundered Doktur.

"The counter!" hissed Larker.

It was now lying on its side and, with the help of Worms, the girl slid it across the floor to block Grunt's path.

THUNK!

"HURR! HURR!" grunted Grunt, which meant "no". Grunt's language is quite simple really. It is only when he grunts three times that things become complicated. He tripped over the counter and fell to the ground.

DOOF!

"HURR! HURR! HURR!" he grunted. What that meant was anybody's guess, but Grunt did not sound pleased.

"Quick! Let's make a run for it!" hissed Larker.

She grabbed Worms by the hand, and together they hurried back up the spiral staircase.

TRIP! TRAP! TROP!

"SLUG MONSTER!" commanded Doktur. **"AFTER THEM!"**

"GURGLE!" gurgled the slug in reply.

"That giant slug won't make it up the stairs," said Worms.

"Don't look back! Just run!" snapped Larker.

But as they ran up the staircase, she noticed a trail of silver painting the wall of the cave.

"Oh no!" she exclaimed.

The **SLUG MONSTER** was using his super-suction powers to stick to the wall. In no time, he had outrun them, or outslithered* them, and was at the top of the staircase, waiting...

"What did the slug say as he slipped down the wall? How slime flies!"

---

* *A word that you won't find in a normal dictionary; only the* **Walliamsictionary** *has this – and a billion other silly words.*

"Not now!" exclaimed Worms.

Larker looked down. At the bottom of the staircase, Doktur was waiting for them.

"You aren't getting away, whoever you are!" purred the teacher.

"We're trapped!" said Worms.

"There must be a way out!" replied Larker.

The **SLUG MONSTER** at her feet opened his mouth and gurgled.

"GURGLE!"

"That thing is going to eat us!" hissed Worms, taking a cowardly step behind Larker. "And you first!"

"My friend is in there somewhere!" she replied.

The **SLUG MONSTER** began sliding straight towards her.

"You are not a monster," began Larker, trying to sound calm despite the deep sense of dread she was feeling. Her heart was pumping so fast she could barely catch her breath.

The monster's tentacles twitched.

"Your name is Spod, and you are my friend. Why exactly? **Dunno!**"

The tentacles twitched again. Larker slowly reached out her hand towards the creature.

"Careful!" whispered Worms from the safety of his hiding place behind her.

Her fingers reached one of the giant slug's tentacles. She stroked it. The monster's expression seemed to soften.

"Spod. Please. Let us pass," she whispered.

"**DESTROY THEM!**" barked Doktur as she raced up the staircase, followed closely by a huffing and puffing Grunt. "**You are my creation, SLUG MONSTER, and you will do what I say! DESTROY! AT ONCE!**"

The creature lifted his head. Whatever kindness he may have had in his expression was gone. It was replaced by a look of evil.

"GURGLE!" he gurgled,

before lunging at Larker.

"ARGH!"

she screamed.

Chapter 29
MIDNIGHT

Worms just managed to whisk Larker up in the air in time. He swung her by her hands over the top of the **SLUG MONSTER**...

WHOOSH!

...before he leaped over too.

The monster snapped at Larker and bit off her boot.

"OUCH!"

He spat out the boot, which began tumbling down the stone stairs.

THONK!

THUNK!

"My boot!" she hissed.

"Leave it!" said Worms.

As the **SLUG MONSTER** launched himself at them, Worms just managed to slam the door behind him.

BANG!

Without looking back, Larker and Worms raced through the vaults of the castle. It wasn't until they were out in the courtyard that they paused for breath.

"I have seen some big slugs in me time," began Worms, "but that one takes the biscuit!"

"What is the definition of a slug? A snail with a housing problem!" said Larker. "We need to stop Doktur and Grunt before they transform any other kids into monsters."

A thick fog was descending on the island.

"Well, it's been a thrilling evening, hasn't it, **Wormy?**" said Worms, taking the worm out of his pocket and kissing her on one end. Let's pray the good end. "But **Wormy** and me better go back to the shed and get some sleep. Goodnight!"

"SLEEP!" exclaimed Larker.

"Shush! You'll wake up the entire school!"

"Sleep!" she exclaimed, a little quieter this time, but not quiet enough for Worms's liking. He grimaced and placed his fingers where he imagined Wormy's ears might be. "How can you sleep at a time like this?"

"What time is it?" he replied, looking up at the pelican chained to one of the turrets.

The pelican was being prodded again by Meddle's mop and squawked twelve times.

"SQUAWK! SQUAWK! SQUAWK! SQUAWK! SQUAWK! SQUAWK! SQUAWK! SQUAWK! SQUAWK! SQUAWK! SQUAWK! SQUAWK!"

Larker and Worms hid in the shadows from the caretaker.

"Twelve squawks! It's midnight!" whispered Worms.

"Now I really feel like Cinderella."

"What?"

"I lost my boot and it's midnight! Hey, why is Cinderella so bad at football?"

"I don't know, but I've got a feeling you're going to tell me!"

"Because she is always running away from balls!"

Worms smiled weakly. "Not one of your best."

"Only Cinderella joke I know. Now, what if Doktur and Grunt find my boot?"

"It's very dark down in that there cave."

"But what if they do?"

"Well…"

"If they find it, they'll know it was me down there."

"We can't go back for it. Not now."

"No."

"It is too dangerous. Let's make a plan in the morning. Right now, it's way past me, your and **Wormy's** bedtime. Goodnight!"

The gardener turned to go, but Larker was having none of it.

"STOP!" said the girl. She was only twelve, but she could be very forceful when she wanted to be. Worms stopped in his tracks.

"One question I'm dying to know the answer to is who is in charge here at **THE CRUEL SCHOOL?**"

"That'll be the headmistress. Always has been and always will be. Been here since the day I arrived as a young whippersnapper!"

"So let's go and see her!"

"See the professor?" he asked. His tone of voice suggested that this was the most absurd suggestion he'd ever heard in his life.

"Yes!" replied the girl.

"But no one has seen the professor for years."

"Why not?" asked Larker, incredulous.

"Well, nobody knows. But the professor has had a **DO NOT DISTURB** sign on her office door forever, and no one has dared to disturb her."

"Tell me where her office is, and I am going to disturb her right now and tell her what is going on!"

"It's midnight! Do you want to get a **DETENTION?**"

A shiver ran down Larker's spine. "No."

"Let's try first thing in the morning."

"Promise?"

"I promise. But the door is always locked. So if she doesn't answer the door then I am sorry, but we don't have a chance."

"Who has the key?"

"It's an old brass one, bigger than all the rest. Meddle must have it."

"Splendid!"

"What do you mean, 'splendid'?"

"Nothing!"

"Don't get yourself into any trouble, missy!" he pleaded.

"As if I would!" she chirped.

Worms shook his head in

despair.

Chapter 30
THE DISAPPEARING SHED

"**S**QUAWK!"

The pelican signalled that another terrible day at **THE CRUEL SCHOOL** was about to begin. Larker lay on her bed, listening out for the caretaker and that **JINGLE! JANGLE! JONGLE!** of his keys. She heard them echoing down the hallway and instantly leaped to her feet.

Meddle unlocked Larker's door and stood in the doorway, the jumble of keys hanging from his belt.

KERCHUNK!

Larker seized her chance. She hurled herself at the caretaker and grabbed him tight. Her eyes were right where the keys dangled.

"WHAT DO YOU THINK YOU ARE DOING?" he thundered.

"Thank you so much for being the best caretaker in the world!" she exclaimed.

"GET OFF ME! OFF! OFF! OFF! WHAT'S WRONG WITH YOU?"

"Nothing! I just thought you needed a hug and someone to tell you what a **wonderful** job you are doing here, making us kids all feel s-o-o-o-o welcome."

"I DO NOTHING OF THE SORT!"

Then, as quickly as Larker had hugged him, she let go and took a pace away from him.

"Goodbye!" she said.

"What do you mean 'goodbye'?"

"You can go now. Goodbye!"

"You are bonkers!"

"And you are too kind!"

The girl's hand was closed tight. As she left her room, she allowed herself a **secret** smile.

Next, instead of following the pack of kids to the dining hall, Larker peeled off in search of Worms.

However, when she pitched up at his shed, she realised something diabolical had happened during the night.

The shed wasn't there!

It had been perched on the edge of the cliff. Now it was gone. Looking down at the ground, she could see a large patch of earth marking its spot.

"A shed doesn't just disappear!" she said to herself.

Larker peered down over the edge of the cliff. To her horror, she spotted shards of wood scattered over the rocks below. It was a very long way down, the length of a couple of football pitches at least, and the shed must have exploded upon impact. Now the cruel sea was claiming it.

SWOOSH!

There was no way anyone could survive that fall.

As the dawn sun rose over the sea, beads of tears welled in the girl's eyes.

"Oh. No. This is too much. I can't take any more. Not poor lovely Worms!"

"Yes?" came a voice from behind her. "Can I help you?"

"ARGH!" she screamed and leaped back.

It was only Worms, but Larker had leaped so far back, she'd lost her balance. Frantically, she waved her arms in the air like a bird who's just hatched trying to take flight for the first time.

"HELP!" she cried, feeling herself tumbling backwards.

Fortunately, Worms shot out his grubby hand just in time and grabbed Larker by her collar.

"GOTCHA!" he exclaimed.

Slowly he pulled her back to safety.

Once they'd taken a few steps away from the edge of the cliff, the girl said, "I thought you were dead!"

"I thought you were dead too!" came the reply.

"We are both still alive!"

"Just!"

"What happened to your shed?"

"Well," began the gardener, "Wormy often needs to take a little widdle during the night." He fished his pet worm out of his pocket. "Sometimes she wakes me up three or four times. So, as luck would have it, I was out giving Wormy her night-time widdle in the bushes over there, you know, to give her some privacy – I can't go if someone's looking!"

The girl rolled her eyes. This man was bananas!

"I heard me shed crash on the rocks below, with all me precious belongings in it."

"Oh no. Poor you. What was in there?"

"Me tea mug."

"Anything else?"

Worms thought for a moment.

"No," he replied.

"Oh. So your mug got broken too."

"Me mug was already broken. The handle had come off. But there's little hope for it now…" he muttered, peering over the edge of the cliff.

"No. Poor mug. Did you see anybody out here last night?"

"There was a thick fog last night, remember? So, no."

"But how else could the shed end up all the way down there?"

"A freak gust of wind?"

"Or something more sinister!" said Larker. "Come on. Let's not waste any more time. Let's go straight to the headmistress and tell her EVERYTHING!"

"What about your boot?"

"My boot can wait!" said Larker, limping off with one boot on and one boot off.

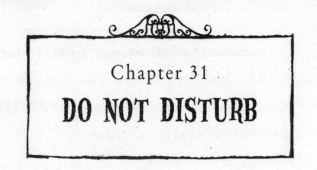

Chapter 31
DO NOT DISTURB

The headmistress's office was tucked away high up in one of the turrets of the castle. Worms and Larker crept up the stone staircase to the top, dodging the rats. Just as Worms had said, there was a sign on the headmistress's door that read:

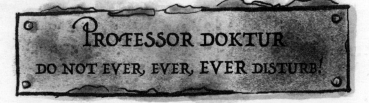

PROFESSOR DOKTUR
DO NOT EVER, EVER, EVER DISTURB!

The sign had been hanging there for so long it was furry with dust.

"I'm pretty sure it's telling us not to disturb," whispered Worms.

"I know!" snapped Larker. "But that sign looks like it's been on her door for decades. It is about time someone disturbed her! Why is her name 'Doktur' too?"

"Professor Doktur is Doctor Doktur's mother."

"So that's how her daughter got the job here!"

"I am sure."

"Why isn't she called Professor Professor?"

"That would be silly."

"I know lots of Doctor, Doctor jokes, but I have never heard of a Professor, Professor one!"

"Doktur Senior became a professor, but Doktur Junior only managed to be a doctor."

"And had to be called Doctor Doktur!"

"Well, go ahead and knock, then, if you really, really want to," said Worms. "And I will wait round the corner just in case she really, really, really doesn't want to be disturbed."

"You work here! You can knock!" replied Larker. "I am not knocking!"

"Somebody's got to knock!"

"Yes! You!"

Larker sighed with frustration. "HMMM!" Then

after a few moments she suggested, "How about we knock together?"

"Good plan!" exclaimed Worms. "You first!"

"No! Together. One! Two! Three! KNOCK!"

KNOCK! KNOCK!

After half a second, Worms hissed, "The professor's not in! Come on! Let's go!"

"We should go in and look for her."

"No, we should not! And, what's more, we can't! We don't have the key!"

Larker smiled and opened her hand. "Oh yes we do!"

There in her sweaty little palm was the big brass key.

"Where did you get that from?" he demanded.

"I… erm, borrowed it from Meddle."

"'Borrowed' it?"

"Yes. I would never steal. I'm going to return it at the earliest opportunity!"

Larker wasted no time and unlocked the old wooden door.

C L I C K !

CREAK!

The door swung open to reveal a study that at first sight looked as if it were covered in snow. Except it wasn't snow. It was thick with dust and cobwebs.

"Seriously spooky!" whispered Larker.

Right on cue, a bat flew straight towards her face. "EEK!"

"URGH!" she cried as it flapped past her and escaped out of the study.

"Let's go!" hissed Worms.

"Go? We've only just got here!" replied Larker.

Immediately, she began tiptoeing around the office. There were piles and piles of paperwork, an old oil painting of the smiling professor with a sour-faced Doctor Doktur when she was just a girl and a globe depicting the solar system, which Larker thought was super cool.

SCRATCH! SCRATCH!

"SHUSH!" she shushed.

"What?" hissed Worms.

"I can hear something!"

"Probably a rat!"

Then a ghostly voice came from seemingly nowhere. "It's not a rat! It's me.

The professor!"

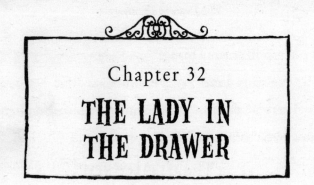

Chapter 32
THE LADY IN THE DRAWER

Larker and Worms trembled with fear. Was the headmistress a ghost?

"Where are you?" called out the girl.

They couldn't see her anywhere in the study.

"I am in here!" said the voice.

"Where?" demanded Larker. "We can't see you anywhere!"

"Here!"

Then there followed a tapping sound.

TAP! TAP! TAP!

"I am in the cabinet!"

It's not at every school that you might find your head teacher in a cabinet. But then **THE CRUEL SCHOOL** wasn't every school.

On one side of the headmistress's study was a tall

wooden cabinet. There were twenty-six drawers, one for each letter of the alphabet. One by one, Larker and Worms began springing them open. Most were jammed full of paperwork that looked as if it had been rammed in at random. Exam papers, report cards and timetables were stuffed in with no regard for filing.

However, one of the drawers contained an old lady! The trick was finding which one.

All the while, as they searched, the headmistress could be heard calling out directions.

"Up a drawer! Down a bit! Left! Left again! Right! Cold! Cold! Tepid! Warmer! Very Warm! BOILING!"

Finally, Larker found the right drawer. On yanking it out, she saw a wrinkly white-haired old lady blinking at the daylight.

"Jolly super to see you!" chirped the headmistress, her pale shrunken head poking out from under a pile of paperwork. It was as if the old school score cards were her bedding. "Are you a new girl?"

"Very new, yes, Professor!" replied Larker. "If you don't mind me asking, what are you doing in the drawer?"

"I don't know," she replied. "I remember nodding off. And time must have marched on! What year is it?"

"You haven't been seen for a decade, Professor!" chipped in Worms.

"Oh! Hello, Worms! I didn't see you there. Well, it must have been an awfully long snooze!"

Larker and Worms shared a look of utter disbelief.

"If you wouldn't mind helping an old girl out?" asked the professor.

"Yes, yes, of course!" replied Larker.

She carefully lifted the impossibly old lady out of the drawer. It was as if she were handling a precious antique, which, in a way, she was. The lady could have been a grandfather clock, as Larker noticed the familiar sound of **ticking** as they lifted her.

TICK! TOCK! TICK! TOCK! TICK! TOCK!

"So, how can I help you both this fine and dandy day?" she asked.

"Well, er, it is hard to know where to begin…" spluttered Larker, looking to Worms for encouragement.

The gardener kept his mouth firmly shut.

"Begin at the beginning! Oh, goody goody! The prof does love stories!"

"Right, well, let me begin with the exploding boy..." began Larker.

She rattled through the story so far. Bug shooting up through the library ceiling. The secret cave under the school. The **MOnsterfication Machine.** The **slug MONSTER.** Worms's shed being pushed off the cliff. It all seemed like some tall tale, but was completely and utterly true.

She concluded, "That's why we knocked on your door, Professor. We desperately need to help all the poor children here before it's too late!"

"You are right! Something must be done! At once!" exclaimed the professor.

The old lady went to stand up, but her leg fell off.

CLUNK!

"I didn't know you had a false leg!" said Worms.

"Nor did I," replied the professor.

Worms and Larker shared a concerned look.

"Would you like us to help put your leg back on?" asked Larker.

"No. No. No fuss, please. Just pop it in a drawer so I don't trip over it!"

Worms shrugged and did what the professor asked. He picked up the metal leg and put it in the cabinet.

"I put it under 'L' for 'leg'!" he said helpfully.

"Thank you, Worms. Well, young lady," continued the professor, "what you have told me about the goings-on here at **THE CRUEL SCHOOL**, especially all that involving my daughter, Doctor Doktur, is absolutely shocking!"

"What should we do?" asked Larker.

"Put down some slug-repellent powder for a start!"

"He was a really big slug!" said Worms.

"Then we need a really big tin of slug-repellent powder!"

"We can't do that! He's my friend! What about your daughter?" asked Larker. "I'm sorry to say that she seems to be behind all this."

"Let me give that girl of mine the sternest of stern

talkings-to! Now you two run along, and please keep all this under your hat!"

"I'm not wearing a hat," remarked Worms, looking up at the mop of hair on his head.

"I mean 'don't tell a soul'. And do close the door on your way out! **Toodle pip!**

Toodle pip!

Toodle pip!

Toodle pip!

Toodle pip!"

Chapter 33
A CIRCUS OF STINKS

Larker and Worms left the headmistress's office even more confused than before.

What was the professor doing sleeping in a drawer?

How did she not know she had a false leg?

And why did she keep saying **"Toodle pip"** over and over again?

"Do you really think she is going to tell her daughter off?" asked Larker as they made their way back down the maze of stone steps and passageways.

"The professor has always been a nice lady," replied Worms. "I don't think she's in on it. She always wanted this school to help children like me so they could behave better and eventually be sent back home."

"So, what went wrong?"

"Everything went wrong when her daughter arrived."

"SQUAWK!" came the sound of the pelican from across the turrets.

"You need to run along to your first lesson, or questions will be asked…"

"With only one boot? What if I run into Doctor Doktur or Grunt?"

"We can launch a rescue mission for your boot at nightfall. In the meantime, you can borrow one of mine," said Worms, yanking off one of his boots.

"That's very kind of you! But it's hardly a match, is it?" she said, looking down at her little brown boot and his huge wellingtons. "It might make people more suspicious. And, anyway, my stupid boot is nothing compared to my friend Spod. It's him we have to save!"

"He's already been turned into a giant slug! It's impossible."

"Nothing is impossible!" said Larker.

"Let's meet again tonight at midnight."

"If we must," he muttered.

"We must! See you later."

With that, the girl hopped down the stone staircase. When Larker reached the bottom of the stairs, she found herself stepping on something unfamiliar. It was only when she looked down that she realised she was standing on a rope net. In an instant, the net was whisked up into the air.

" ARGH!"

she cried.

Looking down, she saw Meddle with his hands on the end of the rope.

JINGLE! JANGLE! JONGLE! went his keys.

"What have I done to deserve this?" pleaded Larker.

"Think you can steal one of my keys, do you?" he said.

"I don't know what you mean!" she lied.

"Liar!"

"Lying is something I would never lie about!" Larker replied.

This confused the caretaker for a moment.

"Where is my key to the professor's office?"

"I have absolutely no idea," she replied. "Have you checked the **Lost Property Office?**"

Meddle threw the net with the girl trapped in it over his shoulder.

"Where are you taking me?" she demanded. "I don't want to be late for Gibber's Gabber!"

"Let's take a look at the **Lost Property Office** for

this key, shall we? We might find something else
that's lost, mightn't we?"

"I don't know what you mean."

"Oh, I think you do."

Larker gulped in fear.

Soon they reached the **Lost Property Office.**
Meddle opened the door and, still carrying Larker
in the net, he stepped into the gloom. The office
absolutely stank. The school was a circus of stinks,
but this was the worst:

Dirty
underpants

Old shoes

Rotten apples

Muddy
football
boots

Pongy shorts

Damp
raincoats

A packed
lunch with egg
sandwiches
from twenty
years ago

Smelly
socks

Chewed
pencils

Whiffy
vests

"Well, well, well," began Meddle. "I don't see the professor's key anywhere…"

"What a shame! Well, we best be going."

"Don't you want to look for your missing boot?" teased Meddle. From the tone of his voice, Larker could tell he'd known something all along.

"What missing boot?"

"The one that is missing from your foot."

"Oh! So it is!" Larker pretended. "No, no, I can cope perfectly well with one boot. In fact, I prefer it. Gives my sock a nice holiday."

Meddle chuckled to himself.

"Why are you laughing?" she asked.

"Because I think your boot has been found…"

From out of the gloom of the **Lost Property Office,** there came a sound. "HURR!"

Larker would recognise that grunt anywhere.

It was Grunt!

And he was holding

her other boot!

Chapter 34
TINY-FEET SYNDROME

The next thing Larker knew, she'd been lugged, still in the net, by Grunt to the Science laboratory.

Waiting for her there was Doctor Doktur, perfectly framed by the stained-glass-window portrait of herself behind.

"Well, well, well..." purred the teacher. "It seems that someone was out of their bed in the dead of night! Tut! Tut! Tut!"

"It wasn't me!" lied Larker.

"Well, let's see, shall we? If the boot fits..."

"I have huge-feet syndrome!" cried the girl. "That boot will never, ever fit!"

"Grunt! Put her down on the counter!"

The assistant dropped the girl on to the worktop.

THUMP!

"Ouch! My bottom!" yelled Larker.

"HISS! HISS! HISS!" sniggered the cat on top of Grunt's head.

"And tiny-feet syndrome! So even if it fits—"

Before the girl could say another word, Doktur had slipped the boot on her foot with ease!

"Cinderella!" cooed Doktur. "It's a perfect fit! Congratulations! You shall go to the ball! Or, rather, to DETENTION!"

"No, no!" she pleaded. "Not DETENTION! Anything but DETENTION!"

"Grunt. The spiral spectacles, if you please!"

"**HURR!**" said Grunt. He reached into his laboratory coat pocket and pulled out the glasses. Grunt turned a little dial on the side so the **spirals spiralled** and **spiralled** and **spiralled**.

W H I R R !

Larker was mesmerised. She couldn't stop staring at the **spirals** as they spun and spun and spun.

W H I R R !

To her HORROR,

Larker could feel herself becoming...

zomb-◎-fied!

PART THREE

THE ARMY OF MONSTERS

Chapter 35
THE BOGEY MAN

The next thing Larker knew, she was chained to a wheelie chair deep down in the secret cave. She had a terrible headache, and it felt as if she'd been asleep for hours. It might already be night-time. There was certainly a chill in the air. However, it was impossible to tell whether it was day or night when you were so far underground.

Larker had the strangest feeling. As much as she wanted to, she couldn't move or cry out. It was as if she were underwater. She had been well and truly **zomb-◎-fied!**

Looking up, she saw that old velvet curtains had been tossed over the semicircle of glass tanks. However, horrifying noises were coming from underneath. They had to be… MORE MONSTERS!

Looking down, she saw that there was another poor victim strapped to the metal table.

WORMS!

The gardener was lying motionless. The evil Doktur and Grunt had **zomb-◎-fied** him too!

The teacher was perusing her cabinet of curiosities. "Mmm. I think we need something extra special for the interfering gardener. Grunt, can you suggest something, please?"

"HURR!" replied her assistant. He then proceeded to root around in his nose with his finger, until he produced the biggest, greenest, slimiest bogey you ever did see.

PLOP!

Fiend's one eye lit up with glee.

"MEOW!"

"Disgusting!" was Doktur's verdict. "I love it! We can call this monster the **BOGEY MAN!**"

Grunt passed the bogey to his mistress as if it were a precious diamond. Doktur took it in her thick black rubber gloves. With great care, she placed the bogey in the **MOnsterfication MaChine**.

If Larker didn't do something fast, her friend Worms was about to become…

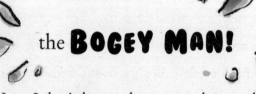

the **BOGEY MAN!**

Now, I don't know about you, dear reader, but the thought of being turned into a giant bogey does not appeal at all.

You would be green for a start!

Worse than being green would be that you'd be sticky!

Worse than being sticky is that you'd be smelly!

There is possibly only one thing worse than being green, sticky and smelly – being called the **BOGEY MAN!**

Seeing Worms in such terrible danger gave Larker a burst of **energy.** It was as if there were a fight going on inside her body to overcome the state in which those **spiral spectacles** of Grunt's had put her. She summoned all her strength, and just managed to cry out,

"STOP!"

Doktur, Grunt and Fiend looked round at this rude interruption.

"Ooh! Sleeping Beauty has finally awoken!" purred Doktur.

"PLEASE! DON'T!" shouted Larker.

"Be patient, child!" hissed Doktur. "Your turn will come soon enough."

"You can't do this!"

"Why ever not?"

"Because I told your mother, the professor, everything! She is on to you!"

The three villains laughed their most villainous laughs.

"HA! HA!"

"HUH! HUH! HUH!"

"HISS! HISS! HISS!"

"Grunt, please fetch my mother," ordered Doktur.

"HURR!"

Grunt nodded and walked over to a corner of the cave. He opened the door to a wardrobe and inside, to Larker's horror, was… the professor.

The headmistress's arms, legs and head must have all fallen off, as they'd been stuck back on to her in all the wrong places. She must be some kind of robot! Her head was where one of her legs should be, and an arm was where her head should be.

"Toodle pip!
Toodle pip!
Toodle pip!"

she kept saying over and over again.

Irritated, Fiend the cat swiped at the headmistress with her one paw.

CLUNK!

The professor collapsed into a pile of metal pieces
on the floor.

KRANKLE!

KRUNKLE!

KRINKLE!

Chapter 36
CLOCKBOTS

"What have you done to the professor?" demanded Larker.

"My mother only ever showed me love, but I always loathed her," replied Doktur.

"Why?"

"I never felt good enough for her. She rose to the giddy heights of professor, something I never could! I was stuck being a humble doctor forever. Can you imagine being called 'Doctor Doktur' your whole life?"

Immediately, Larker sprang to life. This was a joke-teller's dream!

"Doctor, Doctor! I keep thinking I'm a dog! Take a seat. I can't – I'm not allowed on the furniture! Doctor, Doctor! My son has swallowed my pen – what should I do? Use a pencil till I get there.

Doctor, Doctor, I feel like a bell! Take these pills, and if they don't help give me a ring."

"THAT IS ENOUGH!" declared Doktur.

"I could go on like that all day!"

"Grunt, put on the **spiral spectacles!**"

The assistant reached into his coat pocket.

"No! No!" protested Larker. "No more jokes! For now, at least. But tell me this: why is your mum a robot?"

"I was coming to that. When I was young, I was thrown out of Science school for conducting my own special experiments. Experiments on creatures I conducted in the dead of night. Mother gave me one last chance by making me the Science teacher here at THE CRUEL SCHOOL. But when she found out that I was carrying out experiments on the children here she was horrified. She said I had to leave the island immediately, so I had no choice."

"No choice to do what?" asked a spooked Larker.

"So I put on the **spiral spectacles** and put Mother in a trance. Then with the help of Grunt here we carried her up from her bedroom to the roof of the castle."

"Don't tell me you…?" gasped Larker.

"We placed Mother in the cannon. Then Grunt here lit the fuse and KABOOM! She was blasted into the night sky."

"Oh no. Where did she end up?"

"Mother went into orbit as far as I know. She always was fascinated by outer space, so I like to think she finally got her wish to see it up close!"

Grunt smiled in agreement, flashing his metal teeth.

"That's horrendous!" exclaimed Larker.

"It felt horrendously good! But there was a problem."

"You felt bad?" guessed Larker.

Doktur looked puzzled at the thought. "No, no. I felt no guilt. None whatsoever."

"That's reassuring!"

"The problem was how could I explain my mother's absence? She was the headmistress of THE CRUEL SCHOOL, after all. So, using all I'd learned from making clockwork toys as a child…"

"Just like the animal ones in your laboratory!"

"Exactly. I created a clockwork robot of my mother. I called it a '**clockbot**'!"

"**Clockbot?**"

"Genius, isn't it? A metal skeleton covered with a skin made of wax. A moving waxwork all dressed up in her clothes. I found the staff and pupils were easily fooled at first, until she kept falling to pieces. So I hid Mother's **clockbot** in a drawer. Soon after that, I perfected my **clockbots**, and I got greedy."

"Greedy?"

"Questions were still being asked. So anyone at THE CRUEL SCHOOL who got in my way suffered the same fate. KABOOM! Blasted into orbit."

"So all the staff here are robots!" exclaimed Larker.

"**CLOCKBOTS!** Finally, someone has figured it out!"

"So that is why I could always hear the **ticking!**" said the girl. "And why Digits has a metal hand and foot!"

"I trusted Grunt here with the fingers and toes. He miscounted."

Grunt grunted in agreement. "HURR!"

"But why turn everyone into **clockbots?**"

"The **clockbots** do my bidding. With them, I have complete control of THE CRUEL SCHOOL!"

"Why would you want that?"

"My mother's dream was for all the children who were sent here to learn their lesson and be returned to their schools and homes. Goody, goody gumdrops! When I came here as Science teacher twenty years ago, I realised that on this remote volcanic island I was in the perfect place to conduct my dark and dangerous experiments, far away from the prying eyes of the world. Here I invented my masterpiece! The **MOnsterfication Machine!** Grunt, the curtains, please!"

The assistant took his place by the first tank, ready for the big reveal. He grinned proudly, showing off his metal teeth.

"I have been looking forward to this bit!" announced Doktur. "Prepare to be **horrified!**"

Chapter 37

MONSTERS, MONSTERS AND MORE MONSTERS

"**B**ehold my genius creations!" announced Doktur. "Humble Spod, as you know from your late-night adventures, has been turned into…"

Grunt whipped off the first curtain.

"THE **SLUG MONSTER!**"

The giant slug's sticky underside was pushed up

against the glass. Slime was smeared all over the tank.

"And Bug, of course, you saw shooting through the sky. What else would you expect from…"

Grunt whipped off the next curtain.

"METEOR MAN!"

Inside the tank, the monster was burning red and gold, his flames blackening the glass.

"But I have created some new monsters too. Like you, Daft found herself in DETENTION! She was put through the MOnsterfication MaChine with a dinosaur bone, and she became..."

The curtain was yanked off.

"DINO GIRL!"

Larker was horrified to see this new monster. Inside the tank was a creature who was half girl and half dinosaur, with a great big horn sticking out of her head, which she was pounding against the glass.

C R A C K !
CRACK! CRACK!

"A similar fate awaited Pongo!" continued Doktur. "I selected a shark tooth for him for the **MOnsterfication MaChine**, and now he will forever be known as..."

Right on cue, Grunt pulled off the next curtain. Each time, he became a little bit more theatrical, clearly relishing his role.

"SHARK BOY!"

There was no water inside the tank, but this half boy, half shark was swimming around in the air, snapping his terrifying jaws.

SNAP! SNAP! SNAP!

Larker slid down in her wheelie chair. Anything to get further away from the beast.

"Now, Larker," said Doktur, "do you know what an amoeba is?"

"No."

The teacher sighed. "I knew you never listened in

Science class. An amoeba is a single-cell organism that can reproduce by splitting into two."

"Sounds boring," remarked the girl.

"Well, amoebas are a bit boring – not much conversation – but when Knuckles was put through the **MOnsterfication MaChine** with an amoeba, the girl was transformed into..."

The curtain came down, this time landing on Grunt's head.

"THE **ATOMIC AMOEBA!**"

Inside the tank was the strangest sight Larker had seen so far. Behind the glass, a tiny Knuckles, the size of a hamster, was splitting into two! Then those two Knuckleses were splitting into two. Now there were four of her! Then eight! Then sixteen! Then it was impossible to keep count!

"And last but certainly not least," said Doktur, "that deafening girl Boom. I have turned her into a creature that makes no sound whatsoever."

Grunt went to pull the last curtain.

"Not yet!" thundered Doktur. "You will ruin the surprise!"

"HURR!" grunted Grunt.

Fiend gave the man a thwack on his head with her paw.

THWUCK!

"So Boom has been monsterfied into..."

Grunt stood there motionless.

"Now, for goodness' sake!"

"HURR!"

The curtain was whisked down to reveal...

"THE GIANT JELLY!"

Boom was a humongous monster who was half girl and half jellyfish. Behind the glass of the tank, she looked as if she'd been inflated and turned purple.

The monster was squelching up and down, trying to escape.

"What you have done to these kids is soooooo evil!" spluttered Larker.

"Thank you," replied Doktur, beaming with pride. "But that's not all. With these monsters at my side, I will have power beyond your imagination. Soon every child here at **THE CRUEL SCHOOL** will be turned into a monster! Then I can take my **MOnsterfication Machine** away with me, and turn every child in the world into a MONSTER!"

"But I still don't understand why you are doing all this!"

"BECAUSE I HATE CHILDREN!" she bellowed.

"'Hate' is a strong word," replied Larker.

"DETEST! DESPISE! LOATHE! ABHOR! SCORN! SPURN!"

"All right! All right! I think I get the general gist. You don't like kids that much…"

"ALL CHILDREN ARE REVOLTING LITTLE BEASTS WHO SHOULD BE MADE TO SUFFER

FOR ALL ETERNITY!"

"Even me?" asked the girl.

"ESPECIALLY YOU!"

"But you forget you were a child once, Doctor Doktur," said Larker softly, hoping to appeal to the lady's better nature.

Unfortunately, there wasn't one.

"YES! And I was a nasty little brute. Always being beastly to other children, animals and the elderly. I should have been blasted into space at birth!"

"Well, now you say it, that would have been a good plan!"

Doktur's eyes narrowed. "How hilarious you are!"

"You can't do this to us kids! Together we can defeat you!"

"There is no 'together' with these rotters at THE CRUEL SCHOOL. They are all out for themselves. Now that my genius invention of the MOnsterfication MaChine is perfected, my band of monsters will become an army. And your friend the gardener is next!"

"So Worms is the only grown-up here at **THE CRUEL SCHOOL** who isn't a robot?"

"Yes. Apart from me, of course. I was coming to Worms. He was last on my list as he is a mere gardener. But after all that sneaking around with you, uncovering my masterplan, I think he deserves a fate

far worse

than

death..."

Chapter 38
THE SUPERPOWERS OF SNOT

"To be turned into a giant bogey?" asked Larker.

"Exactly!"

"Hey, what's the difference between bogeys and broccoli?"

"Is this a joke?"

"Yes. And you are kind of spoiling it for me."

Doktur sighed. "I don't know. What is the difference between bogeys and broccoli?"

"Kids don't eat broccoli!"

"That's not the least bit amusing."

"It is!"

"I am going to enjoy turning you into a monster!" said the teacher as she paced over to her cabinet of curiosities. "Now, Miss Larker, what would you like to be?"

Doktur's beady eyes scanned over the contents:

A rat's skull

A MOUNTAIN OF MAGGOTS

RHINOCEROS DROPPINGS

A LEECH

A TIGER'S TOOTH

A GLASS EYE (OWNER UNKNOWN)

A FURBALL (NO DOUBT COUGHED UP BY FIEND)

A LARGE GLOBULE OF EARWAX

A BIG, FURRY SPIDER

A SCORPION'S TAIL

"**HURR! HURR! HURR! HURR! HURR!**" grunted Grunt.

"**You are quite right, Grunt!**" replied Doktur, seeming to have understood every word her laboratory assistant had said. "**Let's not get ahead of ourselves. We haven't finished with the bothersome gardener yet. Your partner in crime!**"

"NO!" shouted Larker.

"**Perhaps you would like to take his place?**" asked Doktur.

The girl shook her head. As much as she liked Worms, she had no desire to be turned into a giant bogey.

"But why are you going to turn him into a giant bogey, exactly?" asked Larker, not unreasonably.

"**So this monster of mine will have the superpowers of snot!**" declared Doktur.

Larker looked puzzled, as did Grunt, whose expression rarely changed from one of menace.

"What exactly are the superpowers of snot?" asked Larker.

Grunt nodded his head. He was eager to know too. Even Fiend nodded in agreement.

"Well," spluttered the doctor. She seemed less sure of herself than usual. "The **BOGEY MAN** will be sticky!"

"Big fat deal," remarked Larker. "Glue is sticky!"

"Yes! I know glue is sticky!" snapped Doktur. "But is glue green?"

"No," replied Larker as Grunt shrugged.

"Aha!" cooed Doktur. "I have you there!"

"Being green isn't a superpower!" reasoned the girl. "You are just green. Anyone could paint themselves green. You would just think they were a giant Brussels sprout!"

"Bogeys are also smelly!"

"Mine aren't!" replied Larker.

"You just can't smell them because they are stuck up your nose!"

"Well, I would have thought that would be the perfect place to smell them!" exclaimed Larker. She turned to Grunt and pulled a face. He nodded in agreement.

"HURR!"

Fiend nodded too.

"**SILENCE!**" shouted Doktur. "Grunt! Let's turn this grubby little man into a monster!"

As Larker struggled in vain to wrestle free from the chains holding her down in the wheelie chair, the evil pair went about their work. All this time, Worms had lain motionless on the metal table.

"Lower the greenhouse!" ordered Doktur.

Immediately, Grunt began pulling on the chains.

CLINK! CLANK! CLUNK!

SCHTUM went the greenhouse as it made contact with the floor.

"Now, Grunt, unleash the power of the lava!"

Grunt pulled on a lever and the circular piece of floor slid away.

THUNK!

Once again, the lava lit up the cave red and gold.

Grunt placed the metal tube from the **MOnsterficatiOn MaChine** into the lava.

"Now for my first-ever **BOGEY MaN!**" announced

Doktur. She twiddled with some knobs, pressed some buttons and her precious **MOnsterfication MaChine** whirred into life.

WHIRR!

The light of the force field danced over the greenhouse.

Instantly, Worms began writhing around on the metal counter as his body began changing cell by cell into… SNOT. Every part of him was becoming sticky and green and smelly.

"ARGH!" cried Worms.

"PLEASE! SPARE HIM!" protested Larker.

"**NEVER!**" yelled Doktur.

Just within reach of Larker's big toe was the **DANGER DIAL** on the **MOnsterfication MaChine**. Her only hope to save her friend was to move that dial to push the power to full blast – and with any luck blow up the machine. So she kicked off her boot, reached out her toe and turned the dial all the way to **DANGER! DANGER! DANGER!**

Instantly, the **MOnsterfication Machine** began shaking violently.

RATTLE! RUTTLE! ROTTLE!

Sparks began spraying everywhere as smoke billowed out of the machine.

WHOOF!

"WHAT'S HAPPENING?" cried Doktur.

Grunt ran around, pressing every button, but it was too late.

As for Worms, turning the dial had only made it worse for him. He'd become the biggest, baddest monster of all! With ease, the  broke out of the leather strap that held him to the table.

BURST!

The monster sat up, his head crashing through a pane of the greenhouse glass.

CRASH!

He grabbed hold of the greenhouse and shoved it up to the ceiling.

CLANK!

Next, he hurled the metal table across the cave.

 # CLUNK!

Doktur and Grunt shared a look of BLIND TERROR. Something had gone wrong. Very wrong. Wronger than wrong.

Larker gulped.

Oh no! she thought.

What have I done?

All the other monsters in their tanks were twisting and turning. They could see the **BOGEY MAN** now striding through the cave, causing chaos and destruction.

THUMP!
BOSH!
DOOF!

Larker looked on as the **BOGEY MAN** stomped straight towards his creator.

In fear, Doktur hid behind Grunt, who in turn hid behind her. Then she hid behind him, and then he hid behind her, and so on and so forth, faster and faster and faster, until the pair were nothing more than a blur.

BLUURR!

Now all the other monsters were bashing up against the glass of their tanks.

SLAP!

All were fighting for their freedom.

Larker realised this was her only chance to escape. She reached her feet down to zoom the wheelie chair away as fast as she could.

WHIZZ!

"GRUNT! STOP HER!" barked Doktur.

Fiend curled her tail round the back of the wheelie chair and spun Larker into the centre of the cave.

WHIRR!

The cat did this with such force that the wheelie

chair toppled over and crashed on to the stone floor.

KER-KLANK!

"ARGH!" screamed Larker in pain.

Somehow, the crash dislodged the chains, and the girl could now wriggle out of the wheelie chair. However, as soon as she had, Grunt grabbed her by the ankle and hoisted her off the ground.

"GET OFF ME!" she cried. She swung herself as hard as she could to try to escape his clutches. This caused the hefty Grunt to stumble backwards, slap bang into one of the tanks.

CLUNK!

Grunt knocked into the tank so hard that it toppled over.

DOOF!

This created a domino effect where, in turn, each tank toppled over on to the next.

KERCHUNK!

KERCHUNK!

KERCHUNK!

As the tanks fell to the floor of the cave, the thick glass smashed!

SMASH!

All at once, the monsters were free!

METEOR MAN blazed across the cave, a deadly ball of fire.

The **SLUG MONSTER** slithered out in search of his next victim.

The **ATOMIC AMOEBA** multiplied and multiplied again. Soon there was an army of Knuckleses.

The **GIANT JELLY** squelched up and down.

DINO GIRL let out a mighty roar: "ROAR!"

SHARK BOY circled the cave, chomping at the air.

CHOMP! CHOMP! CHOMP!

Meanwhile, the **BOGEY MAN** was nose to nose with Doktur.

"NO! NO! **BOGEY MAN!** PLEASE! I BEG YOU, NO! I CREATED YOU! I AM YOUR MOTHER!" she shouted.

He reached out and grabbed hold of Doktur and then Grunt.

Still perched on Grunt's head, Fiend tried to bite the **BOGEY MAN,** but the cat became stuck.

"MEOW!" she wailed.

Grunt had not let go of Larker's ankle, despite the girl doing everything in her power to escape, including reaching up and tickling the man's underarm. Needless to say, Grunt did not crack a smile. Now they were all held captive by the **BOGEY MAN.**

"MONSTERS! ATTACK!" cried Doktur. "ATTACK THE **BOGEY MAN!**"

Dino Girl led the charge, lunging at the **BOGEY MAN,** lifting him up off the ground with her long, sharp horn.

He took Doktur, Grunt, Fiend and Larker with him.

All the other monsters had formed a menacing semicircle behind **Dino Girl.**

"Oh dear," sighed Larker. "This isn't my lucky day!"

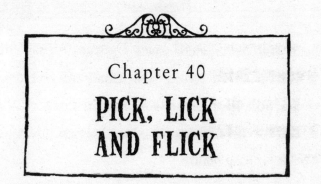

Chapter 40

PICK, LICK AND FLICK

Now, there are three things you have to remember about giant bogeys:

They are green.

They are smelly.

And, most importantly, they are sticky.

A monster like **Dino Girl** is not going to be troubled by the colour green. Nor by the smell. But the stickiness might just be a hazard. And so it proved.

Dino Girl was summoning all her strength to hurl the **BOGEY MAN** across the cave. But, just like one of those sticky boogers that you pick, lick and, try as you might, you just can't flick, she could not get rid of the monster.

Dino Girl swung **BOGEY MAN** above her

head. Still, he remained stuck.

Dino Girl swung him round and round in circles. Still, he stuck on like a limpet.

Dino Girl jumped up and down. The entire cave shook.

RUMBLE!

Whatever **Dino Girl** did, she couldn't unstick the **BOGEY MAN!**

"GRRRR!" growled the half girl, half dinosaur in frustration. As well you might if you couldn't get rid of a giant booger.

Then **Dino Girl** banged her horn against the wall of the cave.

DOOF!

CRUNCH!

The cave wall began crumbling.

"NO, **DINO GIRL,** NO!" ordered Doktur, but it was too late.

Giant rocks began tumbling down on to her, Grunt, Fiend and Larker.

THUD! THUD! THUD!

Rocks swept into the cave like an avalanche.

A cloud of dust exploded.

WOOMPH!

Now was the perfect moment to escape. So, without stopping to say goodbye, Larker raced up the spiral staircase, slamming the invisible door behind her.

SHUNT!

Chapter 41
THE SHADOWS

Larker kept running through the vaults underneath the castle. She was determined to get off this nightmarish island before Doctor Doktur turned her into a monster.

But Larker – being Larker – felt a pang of guilt.

What about her friends still down in the cave? Spod, Bug, Pongo, Knuckles, Daft, Boom and, of course, Worms!

Was there anything she could do to save them?

To her shock, she heard the invisible door open behind her.

CREAK!

Looking over her

shoulder, Larker tripped over the boot of a suit of armour.

CLUNK!

Just as she was about to scramble to her feet, she heard footsteps.

PLOD! PLOD! PLOD!

Looking up from the floor, she could see that a dust-coated Doctor Doktur was leading Grunt and the monsters in pursuit. The only thing Larker could do now was put her head down and pray they didn't see her in the darkness. Fortunately, she was still covered in dust, so there was a good chance she would blend into the shadows.

Larker shut her eyes and scrunched up her body tight, as the footsteps and monster steps grew nearer and nearer. They grew louder and louder…

STOMP! STOMP! STOMP!

…before they became quieter and quieter.

Larker dared to open just one eye. Up ahead, she could see the monsters stomping up the stone steps that led to the castle courtyard.

As silently as she could, Larker rose to her feet. When she was sure they had all gone, she allowed herself a little sigh of relief.

"HHMPH!"

Just at that moment, she felt a hand on her shoulder.

A **giant** hand.

A **green** hand.

A **sticky** hand.

It was the **BOGEY MAN!**

"ARGH!"

screamed Larker.

Chapter 42
STUCK TOGETHER

"**B**OGEY MAN! GET OFF ME!" pleaded Larker.

But the monster brought down his other sticky hand on her other shoulder too.

"GRRRRR!" he growled.

For the first time in her short life, Larker feared she was going to be devoured by a giant bogey.

"PLEASE, **BOGEY MAN!** NO! I BEG YOU!"

The **BOGEY MAN** lifted her off the ground and opened his hideous green mouth wide.

Just at that moment, Larker was sure she spotted a flash of recognition in the monster's eyes.

"WORMS!" she said. "WORMS! DON'T DO THIS! IT'S ME! YOUR FRIEND! LARKER!"

This stopped the monster in his tracks.

"WORMS! PLEASE! I WOULD NEVER,

EVER DO ANYTHING TO HARM YOU!"

The **BOGEY MAN'S** expression softened.

"We are a team! Remember?"

He nodded his head.

"THEN PLEASE PUT ME DOWN!"

The monster did so, carefully setting her on the ground.

"Oh! We are still stuck together!" said Larker. She wiggled as much as she could, but there was no getting away from the giant bogey, so she slipped off her cardigan and left it dangling in his hands.

"You can keep the cardigan. I'm not sure it is your size, though," quipped Larker.

The girl detected a *smile* from the monster.

"WORMS! I knew it! You are still in there somewhere!" she exclaimed. Larker opened her arms to give the monster a hug, but instantly thought better of it. She would only become stuck again.

"Worms, I need your help. I can't do it alone. I'm sure that together we can defeat Doktur, and help all these children escape from this island. Will you help me?"

It was a struggle for the monster, but he just managed to say, "YES!"

"You can speak! Now, you are already a monster, so you have monster powers. But I don't. I'm going to have to make myself into some kind of superhero if I want to defeat this evil villain!"

Larker looked around the vaults. There was several jumble sales' worth of junk down here:

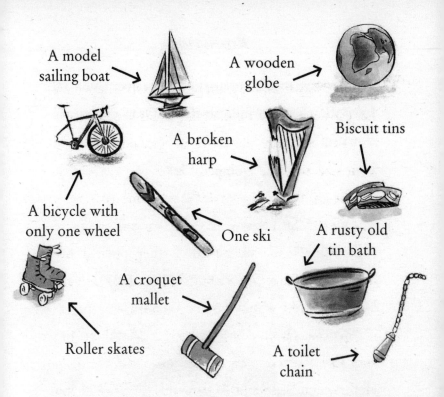

A model sailing boat

A wooden globe

Biscuit tins

A broken harp

A bicycle with only one wheel

One ski

A rusty old tin bath

A croquet mallet

Roller skates

A toilet chain

"Doktur and her band of monsters will be back soon enough when they realise I'm not up there in the castle!" exclaimed Larker. "Let's grab everything we can and hide out somewhere."

"SHED?" suggested the **BOGEY MAN.**

"That's in a hundred pieces bobbing around in the sea, remember?"

"HMMM. YOUR... ROOM?"

"That's the first place they'll look! I know!

Doktur's Science laboratory! She'll never think I'd have the cheek to hide in there! Grab everything you can!"

The **BOGEY MAN,** being a sticky monster, could grab rather a lot. They raced up the stone steps, both of them clutching armfuls of junk.

"I'll need a name, though!" said the girl. "It's not fair that everyone's got a dead cool name except me!"

Chapter 43
GADGET GIRL

So, hiding out in Doktur's Science laboratory, Larker and the **BOGEY MAN** set to work on creating her a superhero outfit. Now it was way past midnight. Lessons had long since ended, and everyone else would be in bed. The stained-glass window of Doctor Doktur loomed over them as they went to work.

The wonderful thing about being in the laboratory was that Larker and the **BOGEY MAN** now had many more toys to play with – not just everything they'd swiped from the vaults, but all the weird and wonderful equipment in the laboratory too.

In no time, Larker looked something like a superhero fit to take on a band of monsters. A home-made superhero, but a superhero all the same.

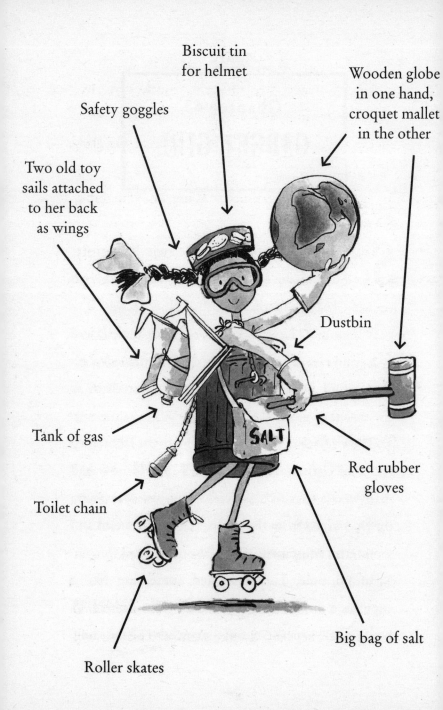

Biscuit tin
for helmet

Safety goggles

Wooden globe
in one hand,
croquet mallet
in the other

Two old toy
sails attached
to her back
as wings

Dustbin

Tank of gas

Toilet chain

Red rubber
gloves

SALT

Roller skates

Big bag of salt

As she made the finishing touches to her superhero outfit by placing a biscuit tin on her head, Larker looked at her reflection in one of the glass cabinets.

"Ta-da!" she exclaimed. "What do you think, **BOGEY MAN?**"

The **BOGEY MAN** shrugged. From his sticky green expression, you could tell he thought the girl looked rather silly.

"Come on! This is cool! The roller skates and air-tank combo means I will zoom along at the speed of light away from the *Giant Jelly!*"

"What about **SHARK BOY?**" asked the **BOGEY MAN.**

"What do you think these are for, bozo?" said Larker, waggling the sails from the model boat. "Wings! To fly!"

"Hmm. What is that for?" he asked, pointing at the globe.

"This will knock out all the **Atomic Amoebas** in one go! They will fly like skittles! This bin will protect me from the flames of **METEOR MAN!** And what do slugs hate?"

The **BOGEY MAN** thought long and hard about this. "Rude waiters?"

"No! Look!"

Larker showed off her big bag of salt.

"Salt!" exclaimed the monster.

"We got there!"

"Why the biscuit tin on your head?"

"I would like to see the half-human, half-dinosaur **Dino Girl** get through this!" she said, clonking it.

CLONK!

Larker clonked a little too hard and the biscuit tin crumpled.

CRUNKLE!

"Ouch! This tin is thick enough to protect pink wafer biscuits! It can surely protect the giant brain of… wait for it!"

"Hmmm?"

"Drum roll, please!"

"Hmmm?"

"GADGET GIRL!"

There was silence.

"Well, do you like my superhero name?" she asked.

The **BOGEY MAN** shrugged.

"It's way cooler than the **BOGEY MAN!**" declared Larker.

The **BOGEY MAN** rolled his sticky green eyes.

But, before they could get into an argument, the girl heard monster steps in the hallway.

STOMP!

STOMP!

STOMP!

"It's them!"

she hissed.

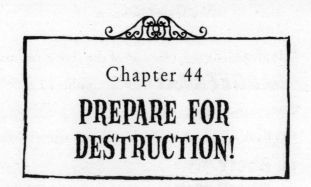

Chapter 44
PREPARE FOR DESTRUCTION!

STOMP! STOMP! STOMP!

The monster steps stopped when they reached the door to Doktur's Science laboratory.

Larker gulped in fear. The monsters were so close she could smell them.

"There's only one way to do this," she whispered.

"How?" asked the **BOGEY MAN**.

"Together."

Just then there was a terrific noise as the door began to be bashed in.

BASH!

BOSH!

BISH!

Larker skated to the far end of the classroom and beckoned for the **BOGEY MAN** to follow her.

Still the door suffered a pounding.

"Did you lock it?" whispered Larker.

The **BOGEY MAN** shook his head.

She called out, "THE DOOR'S OPEN!"

At that moment, the door and part of the wall surrounding it fell into the laboratory.

CRASH!

Standing in the doorway were Doctor Doktur and her trusted sidekick, Grunt, with Fiend, of course, perched on his head. All six of the monsters that the pair had created loomed behind them.

Doktur smirked when she saw the girl all dressed up.

"Who on earth are you meant to be?" she purred.

"GADGET GIRL!" announced Larker. "Trembling, aren't you?"

"Not even a tiny bit."

"Trembling on the inside, I bet! You can run away now, if you like!"

Now Grunt, Fiend and all the monsters were snorting with laughter too. "HO! HO! HO!"

"**HISS! HISS! HISS!**"

"You had your chance," said Larker. "Now, all of you! Prepare for DESTRUCTION!"

With a flourish, she yanked on the toilet chain attached to her backpack. The tank shot out gas.

PFFT!

GADGET GIRL was propelled along the floor on her roller skates…

W H I R R !

…slower than a snail. You'd be forgiven for thinking that she wasn't moving at all.

The sound of the gas escaping from the tank was tragic too.

PFFFT!

It sounded like a bottom burp leaking from an elderly elephant.

"OOPS!" said the **BOGEY MAN.**

"'OOPS' is the word," agreed ***GADGET GIRL.***

"Now, you must prepare for DESTRUCTION!" announced Doktur. "MONSTERS! OBLITERATE THEM!"

The **Atomic Amoeba** was splitting in half again and again and again until there were hundreds of her. There were so many that they blocked the doorway. There was no chance of escape.

The **Giant Jelly** was bouncing not just up and down, but from side to side too. The monster was bouncing so hard that dust and debris were exploding off the walls.

BOINK!

BOINK! BOINK!

KRUNCH!

KABOOM!

K R U N K L E !

Dino Girl roared and lifted her horn high into the air.

"ROAR!"

The **SLUG MONSTER** began sliding across the wall.

Lighting up the hallway was **METEOR MAN**. The scorching heat of the fiery red beast was so intense it felt as if it could set the whole castle ablaze.

WHOOF!

Swishing through the air overhead was the terrifying sight of a flying killer fish... **Shark Boy!**

Sometimes, when faced with grave danger, the best policy is to... RUN AWAY!

REALLY FAST!

RUN AWAY AS FAST AS YOU POSSIBLY CAN!

That is exactly what Larker did. However, she must have forgotten she had roller skates on because when she tried to run she began rolling out of control.

WHIZZ!

"WHOA!" she cried as she crashed straight through the huge stained-glass window of Doctor Doktur.

SHATTER!

Chapter 45
SHOWDOWN!

"**MY WINDOW!**" shouted Doktur. "**MONSTERS! AFTER HER!**"

"**HISS!**" hissed Fiend, digging her razor-sharp claws into Grunt's big bald head.

"**UGH!**" grunted Grunt. This didn't sound like a yes or a no. It sounded like a yelp of pain.

The band of monsters began scrabbling to get through the broken window first.

Thinking fast, the **BOGEY MAN** leaped up on to the ledge and, like a giant spatter of snot, covered the frame.

"**YOU HAVE TO GET THROUGH ME!**" shouted down the **BOGEY MAN,** looking as smug as you could look if you were a giant bogey.

The monsters hesitated, no doubt remembering

what a sticky mess they'd found themselves in down in the cave.

"**ATTACK!**" yelled Doktur.

Fiend lifted her paw in the air to lead the charge.

"**HISS!**"

All at once, Grunt, Fiend and the six monsters surged towards the **BOGEY MAN**...

SQUELCH!

...and instantly all became tangled up in one big, green, gooey mess.

Together they tumbled out of the window and fell to the ground.

DOOMPH!

Larker had landed upside down in a hedge, her roller skates poking out of the top.

She could barely believe her eyes when she saw all six monsters, Grunt and Fiend tangled up together in the giant bogey like...

...ONE **HUGE** MONSTER!

As this giant monster rose to its sticky green feet, it towered over the girl, casting a long, dark shadow from the light of the moon.

Now standing at the window to her laboratory was Doktur.

"BEHOLD!"

she cried triumphantly.

"MY MEGAMONSTER!"

Chapter 46
THE MONSTER TO END ALL MONSTERS

The **MEGAMONSTER** was the monster to end all monsters.

It had three heads on top. One was that of a shark, one of a bogey man and another of a dinosaur. The shark and dinosaur heads were roaring and snapping away at the air, no doubt furious that they were now gummed together by a giant bogey.

One of its arms was the **Atomic Amoeba,** who was, of course, multiplying rapidly.

The other arm had become entangled with **METEOR MAN** and was blazing as hot as the sun.

The belly of the beast was the **SLUG MONSTER,** twisting and turning as he tried to escape.

As for the **BOGEY MAN'S** legs, one side was now entwined with Grunt. Just where the kneecap might be was his big bald head.

If Grunt looked livid, Fiend was fuming! You've never seen a cat so hopping mad with anger.

The list of things cats hate is long:

Baths

Big dogs

Lawnmowers

Fireworks

Being dressed up to look like a baby and paraded around the park in a pram

Deep snow

Being given any kind of medicine

Curdled milk

Being stroked one too many times

Other cats

But there is nothing they hate more than becoming bogeyfied.*

---

* A real word you will find in the world's greatest, but overpriced, reference book, *The Walliamsictionary*.

The other green, slimy leg ended in the most surprising way. Not with a foot, but with a jelly. A **Giant Jelly** to be precise.

"NOW, MY **MEGAMONSTER!** DESTROY THAT WRETCHED GIRL!" ordered Doktur.

Larker tried to untangle herself from the hedge, but being upside down made it almost impossible. Her roller-skated feet might be waggling out of the top of the hedge, but her body was entangled by the branches. As much as she fought against them, Larker couldn't set herself free.

"STOP!" shouted the **BOGEY MAN,** trying to hold himself and all the other monsters back.

The problem was that, even though they were stuck together, they didn't know how to work as a team. They were pulling every which way, snarling and snapping at the night air.

The **MEGAMONSTER** stumbled forward.

THUD!

It was so heavy that the force on the ground launched Larker out of her landing spot and into the air.

WHOO<small>SH!</small>

She landed on her back with a clunk.

CLUNK!

It was hard for Larker to move in her **GADGET GIRL** get-up. It was so cumbersome. For a moment, she lay on the ground with her arms and legs waggling in the air, like an upturned beetle.

"URGH!" she cried in frustration, but she just managed to roll herself over on to her front.

However, just before she could scramble to her feet, she felt herself being plucked off the ground. The **Atomic Amoeba** had the girl in her many, many clutches. She raised Larker into the air. As Larker passed by the **SLUG MONSTER,** she tried to hurl a handful of salt at him, but instead just managed to get it in her own eyes.

"OUCH!"

Still the **Atomic Amoeba** pushed Larker higher and higher into greater and greater danger. Now she was level with the heads at the top of the **MEGAMONSTER!**

"GULP!"

The **BOGEY MAN** was in the middle, with **Shark Boy** and **Dino Girl** on either side. The poor **BOGEY MAN** was being bashed again and again by the shark and the dinosaur. Those two monsters were fighting to see who could gobble up the girl first.

SNAP!

"GRRR!"

"USE WEAPONS!" shouted the **BOGEY MAN**.

"But they might harm you!"

The **BOGEY MAN** shook his head. "DON'T WORRY ABOUT ME!"

So Larker threw the globe into the shark's mouth. Even for a beast like that, a huge wooden globe was too much to swallow. Despite having teeth as sharp as samurai swords, he just couldn't crunch down on it. It was like when a small child goes into a sweetshop and asks for a gobstopper as big as their

head. It might just fit into their mouth, but there is zero chance of them swallowing it!

Just as **Dino Girl** was smirking at **Shark Boy's** misfortune, she was met with the clonk of a croquet mallet on her head.

CLONK!

It knocked the dinosaur out cold.

"YES!" exclaimed the **BOGEY MAN,** his face stuck between the chomping shark and the now snoozing dinosaur.

"HA! HA!" cried Larker.

But if *GADGET GIRL* thought she had the upper hand she was mistaken, because she was about to be

attacked

from

below...

Chapter 47
THE BEAST FROM BELOW

"YEOWW!" cried Larker in agony. Fiend had sunk her fangs through her roller skate and into her foot. The pain was eye-watering. Her foot felt like it was on fire. She swung herself away from the beast, only to find herself in the clutches of **METEOR MAN.** Now, after feeling that her foot was on fire, her foot really *was* on fire!

WHOOMPH!

"YEOWWWW!" she cried again.

The **Atomic Amoeba** swung Larker round and round and round until she was nothing but a blur.

BLLLUUUUURRR!

Then she let go!

WHOOSH!

Larker shot up into the air.

She skimmed the head of the poor pelican chained to one of the turrets.

"SQUAWK!"

"Sorry!" she cried as she shot higher and higher into the sky.

WHOOSH!

Then there was the strangest sensation. Larker could feel herself slowing to a stop.

The only way was down!

She began falling at high speed.

"ARGH!"

W H I Z Z !

Now was the real test of her **GADGET GIRL** costume. Would she be able to fly?

Larker opened her home-made wings, which she'd made from the old model sailing boat.

WHOOMPH!

Instantly, she began gliding through the clouds.

GADGET GIRL was FLYING!

"HA! HA!" she cried, the breeze cooling her hot feet.

"SHOOT HER OUT OF THE SKY!" ordered Doktur from the window of her laboratory.

In a heartbeat, **METEOR MAN** hurled red-hot balls of fire into the sky.

ZOOM!

ZOOM!

ZOOM!

They sizzled as they skimmed past the girl.

SIZZLE!

Then DISASTER STRUCK! One of the fireballs hit **GADGET GIRL'S** wings. Larker looked to her side to see flames devouring one of the sails. Before she could say "Oh, poo!" she found herself spiralling down through the sky.

WHIRRR!

With only one wing and the other on fire, it was impossible to control her speed. Larker was falling at an alarming rate. Using her arms as wings, she could just about set a course.

A collision course!

If she were to end up as human jam on the ground, she was at least going to take out someone with her. That someone was Doctor Doktur.

So she began swooping straight towards the laboratory's window where the evil Science teacher was barking her orders to the **MEGAMONSTER.**

On seeing what the girl was doing, Doktur's beady eyes widened in fear. **"MEGAMONSTER! STOP HER!"** she cried, leaping down from the window frame into her classroom to take cover.

The **MEGAMONSTER** lunged this way and that to try to steer into the girl's flight path. *GADGET GIRL* slammed into the **MEGAMONSTER**.

WHAM!

She slammed so hard that she separated Grunt and Fiend from the rest and sent them zooming through the air.

WHOOSH!

The evil pair parted company for the first time. Both the one-legged cat and the hefty laboratory assistant tumbled through the sky. They zoomed past the castle and over the side of the cliff. Seeing that they were going to plunge into the shark-infested sea below, they tried to take flight. Grunt flapped his big, wobbly arms and Fiend flapped her tail like a windscreen wiper.

FLAP! FLAP! FLAP!

The last anyone heard of them were their cries as they tumbled into the sea.

"HURR!"

"MEOW!"

SPLOSH! SPLASH!

Larker was battered and bruised, but still alive. She spotted the **spiral spectacles** lying on the ground. They must have fallen out of Grunt's laboratory coat. She snatched them and shoved them in a pocket. Then she felt a shadow looming over her. It was the **MEGAMONSTER**.

"Kids! Please!" begged Larker.

"I am not your enemy. I am your **friend!** Remember? It's me! Larker!"

The **MEGAMONSTER** hesitated for a moment.

"If we all work together, then we can defeat the real monster – Doctor Doktur!" she declared. "Spod, you told me that it was every kid for themselves at this school. Well, if that really is the case, then there is no chance. Evil will triumph over good. But I am sure we can be powerful if we all learn to work together. As a team! Isn't that right, Spod?"

The Slug Monster stopped moving. "You are in there somewhere – I know it! Spod! My very first friend at this school, but certainly not my last. Spod! Are you there? And don't say '**dunno**'!"

"Larker?" spluttered the **SLUG MONSTER.**

"Yes! It's me! You gentle giant, you! Be the first to turn good!"

"**Dunno!**"

"No! Don't say '**dunno**'!"

The **SLUG MONSTER** thought again. "YES!"

"YES!" exclaimed Larker. "One down! Five to go! Bug! I know we got off to a bad start, but I promise I will never mention that you shoved toenail-grot jam in my face ever again!"

"That was funny," said **METEOR MAN.**

"I guess it was! Bug, will you be part of our team?"

"Yes!"

"YES!" cried Larker, now turning her attention to the **Giant Jelly.** "Come on, Boom. All this squelching must be fun, but what could be more fun than being the gobbiest girl in the school?"

The **Giant Jelly** bounced up and down in agreement.

"COOL!"

"NOW COME ON, THE REST OF YOU!"

shouted Boom. "Knuckles! Pongo! Daft! Let's do what the new girl says! Let's finally work as a team!"

"What do you say?" asked Larker.

But before she could hear the answer she found herself flying backwards through the air.

WHOOSH!

She flew all the way back towards the laboratory, stopping suddenly with a hard **CLANK!**

The dustbin she had round her middle had become stuck to the powerful electromagnet!

Doktur was at the controls. It was her most precious piece of equipment from her Science laboratory.

"Not so clever now, are we, *GADGET GIRL?*" purred Doktur.

The evil teacher flicked a switch, turning the electromagnet off, and Larker tumbled to the ground.

DOOF!

"Now goodbye, forever!"

With that, Doktur shoved the dustbin round **GADGET GIRL'S** middle as hard as she could.

CLUNK!

Larker began rolling at speed towards the edge of the cliff.

TRUNDLE!

There was nothing she could do to stop! She bounced off a rock...

DOOF!

...and careered off the side of the cliff.

wHOOSH!

"AAARRRRRGHHH!" cried Larker.

Chapter 48
CLIFFHANGER

Larker just managed to dig her fingernails into the earth on the edge of the cliff. She was clinging on for dear life.

The **GADGET GIRL** outfit was heavy, and Larker could feel her fingers slipping. Try as she might, she couldn't heave herself up. Just as she felt her life slipping away from her, she looked down. The mighty sea was raging below. If the rocks didn't batter her, she was sure to drown, or even be eaten by the shiver of sharks that was circling, eager to take a bite of this tasty little morsel.

But just as Larker closed her eyes for what she thought would be the last time she felt her fingers being pushed down into the earth. Larker looked up. It was Doktur treading on her fingers.

"Thank you!" exclaimed Larker. "You saved my life."

Doktur chuckled to herself. "Oh no! I am not saving you. I am savouring you! Savouring this final moment before you meet your grisly end."

"You are the evillest person who ever lived!"

"Thank you so much. I try my best. To think a silly little girl like you could stop my brilliant plan! Now it is time for me to say good..."

Doktur lifted one foot off the ground.

Larker slipped further. "ARGH!" she cried.

Now she was holding on with just one hand. But one by one she could feel her fingers slipping.

"PLEASE! I BEG YOU! DON'T LET ME FALL!"

Doktur smirked. "...bye!"

The evil teacher lifted her other foot off the ground.

Larker's fingers dragged through the earth.

SCRAPE!

And then there was nothing left to hold on to.

Just air.

Larker was falling. Falling. Falling. Falling.

WHOOSH!

"AAARRRGGGHHH!"

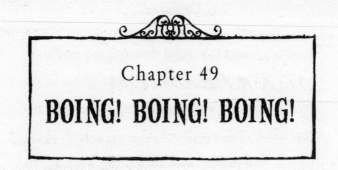

Chapter 49
BOING! BOING! BOING!

As Larker plummeted through the air, she saw the sharks rising out of the waves. Their monstrous mouths were wide open, ready for their dinner to fall straight in.

The girl fumbled with her air tank.

EMPTY!

She tried to stretch out her burnt wings.

BROKEN!

In desperation, she tried flapping her arms.

USELESS!

All that was left to do was shut her eyes and wait for the end.

But the end did not come.

Instead, she felt herself landing on something.

BOING!

Larker opened her eyes.

It was the **MEGAMONSTER!**

"What the…?" she spluttered.

The creature had leaped down on to the rocks and stretched itself out to form a huge green trampoline.

Larker was bouncing up and down, having the time of her life.

"YIPPEE!" she exclaimed. "We are a team!"

"Yes! We are!" chimed in all the creatures of the **MEGAMONSTER,** together.

Looking up, Larker could see the silhouette of Doctor Doktur standing on the edge of the cliff, before disappearing from view.

"But this isn't over yet!" she said. "Come on!"

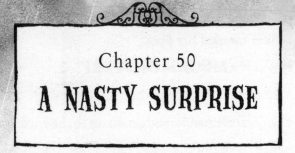

Chapter 50
A NASTY SURPRISE

When they finally reached the top of the cliff, Doktur had vanished.

"Where could she be hiding?" Larker wondered aloud.

The **MEGAMONSTER** scratched its heads.

"Somewhere so obvious that it would be the last place we'd look!" added Larker.

"THE SECRET CAVE!" exclaimed **Dino Girl.**

"DAFT! You are a genius!" replied Larker.

"Am I?"

"YES!"

"What's a genius?"

"It means you are very, very, very clever!"

"WOW!"

"To the secret cave!" ordered Larker, and the **MEGAMONSTER** followed close behind.

They descended the stone steps to the vaults under the castle, and soon reached the invisible door.

When it creaked open, the girl felt a sudden surge of fear. She didn't want to be the first down that long spiral staircase. If Doktur was down there, she was sure to have set a trap.

"Erm, please, after you," spluttered Larker to the **MEGAMONSTER.**

"No! No!" replied the **BOGEY MAN,** speaking

up for all the muttering monsters. "We insist!"

Larker fell silent for a moment. "Can we go together?" she asked.

"YES!" said the **BOGEY MAN,** all the monsters murmuring in agreement.

"I am afraid of the dark."

"Caves give me the willies."

"All hold hands."

"I want my mummy."

"Nobody guff!"

"As if I would!"

When they reached the floor of the cave, Doctor Doktur was nowhere to be seen, although she could easily be hiding behind the fallen rocks.

Larker broke away from the others to sabotage the **MOnsterfiCatiOn MaChine**. She let her fingers run along the wires sprouting from it, then yanked out one marked **"FORCE FIELD"** and plugged it into a different socket. That way, if Doctor Doktur had a nasty surprise in store for them, they would have a nasty surprise in store for her!

Meanwhile, the **BOGEY MAN** took **Wormy** out of his pocket. "All right, my little friend? Are you afraid of the dark?" he cooed, before lifting the creature up to his mouth for a kiss. He kissed both ends, to be sure he'd got it right.

Larker clambered over the rocks to see if she could spot Doktur anywhere, but she couldn't, so she tiptoed over to the **MEGAMONSTER** at the centre of the cave.

"She's not here!" hissed the **BOGEY MAN.** "Let's go."

"I can sense evil down here – I'm sure of it," replied Larker.

Sure enough, suddenly the greenhouse shot down from the roof of the cave.

RATTLE!

In shock, Worms dropped **Wormy** to the ground, and she wriggled away.

The greenhouse landed square on top of Larker and the **MEGAMONSTER,** imprisoning them.

"NOOOO!"

"HELP!"

"LET US OUT!"

"PLEASE!"

"WORMY? WHERE ARE YOU?"

"SOMEONE'S GUFFED!"

"I CAN'T HELP IT! I'M NERVOUS!"

Looking up, Larker spotted a figure standing proudly on the roof of the greenhouse, like a pirate aboard their galleon.

"Did you miss me?" asked Doktur with a snigger.

"HA! HA! HA!"

Chapter 51
SOMETHING STRANGE

"You won't get away with this!" snapped Larker.

"I already have!" replied Doktur. "You can do nothing to stop me. All I need to do now is decide what exactly to turn you all into!"

With the precision of a ballet dancer, she leaped off the roof of the greenhouse and on to the cave floor. Inside the greenhouse, the **MEGAMONSTER** was beginning to panic.

"STOP HER!"

"We can smash our way out!"

"Wormy? Wormy? Where are you?"

"SILENCE!" thundered Doktur. "You are all trapped by the FORCE FIELD."

She yanked on the lever. However, this time, instead of the lightning dancing over the greenhouse, it seemed to dance all over the cave.

FIZZLE! FAZZLE! FUZZLE!

Doktur noticed that this was strange, but ignored it. Her **Monsterfication Machine** was a work of utter genius and would never let her down.

"Now," she began, taking her time to make it as torturous as possible. "What would be the absolute worst thing to be turned into?"

The lady perused all the drawers in her cabinet of curiosities, inspecting her collection of nasties.

"TADPOLES? ROTTEN TEETH? ALBATROSS POOP? MAGGOTS? FURBALLS? UNDERARM JUICE? WOODLICE? EARWAX? CATERPILLARS? FOOT CHEESE? TOADS? SLUDGE? GROT? NASAL HAIRS? SEVERED THUMBS? ROTTEN CABBAGE?"

Then she noticed something crawling across the floor. It was **Wormy** the worm.

"Ah! I have just the thing! A wiggly waggly-worm!"

"NOT **WORMY!** I BEG YOU!" cried the **BOGEY MAN**.

"NO! NO!" yelled Larker. "Don't turn us into worms, please!"

The others all begged too.

"Do or don't?" teased Doktur.

"DON'T!" she screamed.

"Now that you've said 'don't', I definitely WILL turn you all into worms."

"All right!" said Larker, about to take a chance. "Do turn us into worms!"

"It would be a pleasure!" purred Doktur.

"NOOOOO!" cursed the girl, furious with herself for having been tricked.

Doctor Doktur placed the worm into the machine.

"Come along, my little nasty!"

The wicked lady pushed the button on her **MOnsterficatiOn Machine.**

"This will be my most

horrifying creation

yet!"

Chapter 52

MONSTERFICATION

There were shouts from all the monsters.

"NOOOO!"

"NOT A GIANT WORM!"

"PLEASE!"

"THIS IS THE END!"

Above all the hubbub, Larker hissed, "Please be quiet and wait!"

"Wait for what?" spluttered the BOGEY MAN.

"I just tinkered with the wires on the MOnsterficatiOn Machine!" hissed Larker.

"SO?"

"So look at the FORCE FIELD. It isn't over the greenhouse – it's out there!"

"BUT...!"

"SHUSH!" urged Larker.

Just as she thought, nothing was happening to her or the **MEGAMONSTER** inside the greenhouse. Nothing at all. However, outside in the cave was a different story. Right in front of their eyes, Doctor Doktur was turning into a MONSTER!

"NOOOOOOOOOOOOOOO!" screamed Doktur as she became half Science teacher, half giant worm.

Doktur's face was becoming brown and bulbous. Her wormy body burst out of her clothes and she toppled from her feet, which had become a tail.

In a stroke of good luck for Larker and the **MEGAMONSTER,** the **Giant Worm** fell on to the lever that activated the greenhouse.

CLANK! CLUNK! CLINK!

The greenhouse raced up to the ceiling of the cave. It smashed against the rocks.

SMASH!

Deadly shards of glass fell from the ceiling.

W H O O S H !

The **MEGAMONSTER** leaped out of the way just in time, but in all the hurry to flee Larker stumbled and fell forward.

CLANK!

She was falling into the pit of lava.

"NOOOO!" she cried.

Glass daggers rained down on her from the ceiling.

PNANG! PNANG! PNANG!

They pinned Larker down like a knife-throwing act at the circus.

TWONG! TWANG! TWUNG!

Now she was trapped, lying over the lava pit.

The **Giant Worm** was crawling towards her. The creature's mouth opened, ready to gobble her up.

SNARL!

Then the **MEGAMONSTER** leaped into the **Giant Worm's** path.

DOOF!

"JOIN ME, **MEGAMONSTER!**" commanded the **Giant Worm**. "We can rule not just this school but the entire world for all eternity! We can turn every child on the planet into a monster!"

"NO!" replied **MEGAMONSTER,** all the voices of the monsters speaking in unison.

"THEN PREPARE TO BE DEVOURED!"

With that, the **Giant Worm** lunged at the **MEGAMONSTER,** taking a chomp out of its arm.

CHOMP!

METEOR MAN fell to the floor, now free. Summoning all his strength, he blasted a red-hot ball of fire at the **Giant Worm**.

WHOOSH!

The creature dodged out of the way, and the fireball hit the **MOnsterficatiOn MachiNe.**

WHOOMPH!

Instantly, the machine exploded.

KABOOM!

The **Giant WoГm** wailed, "MY LIFE'S WORK IS DESTROYED! NOW YOU TOO WILL BE DESTROYED!"

She lunged again at the **MEGAMONSTER,** taking another huge bite out of it. All she got was a sticky mouthful of bogey and another of the creatures wriggling free. This time it was **Shark Boy's** turn to escape.

"CHOMP! CHOMP! CHOMP! CHOMP!"

Four more chomps from the **Giant WoГm** and not only the **Giant Jelly, Dino GirI** and the **SLUG MONSTER,** but also the **Atomic Amoeba** were now free from the **BOGEY MaN!**

The **Giant WoГm** flailed around, trying to chomp at all the creatures spinning around her. There were more and more by the moment as the

Atomic Amoeba multiplied and multiplied, and multiplied some more.

PING! PING! PING!

The **Giant Jelly** launched herself at the **Giant Worm,** landing as hard as she could on to her tail.

THONK!

"EURGH!" came a guttural growl of pain from the **Giant Worm.** She whipped her tail as hard as she could...

SNAP!

...sending the **Giant Jelly** flying through the air. The monster hit the spiral staircase...

THUMP!

...sending it crashing to the ground.

SMASH! CRASH! WALLOP!

Now there was no way out of the secret cave!

Chapter 53
GOBBLED UP

To make matters worse, Larker was about to be gobbled up by a giant worm. Her fate was to become worm food — flame-grilled worm food because the heat from the lava was cooking her! Her only means of escape was to free herself from these shards of glass that were pinning her over the lava pit. But, try as she might, they just wouldn't budge.

"URGH!" she cried as she struggled.

"You started this revolution, Larker. Now it will end! Forever!" announced the **Giant Worm,** opening her mouth to take her first deadly bite out of her.

Just then Larker remembered she still had the **spiral spectacles** in her pocket. With difficulty, she put them on and pressed the button on the side.

"NO! NO!" shouted the **Giant Worm**.
"Not the **spiral spectacles!**"

Under the gaze of the **spiral spectacles**,
the **Giant Worm** became dead still. Then she
began falling straight towards the girl. They
were both about to tumble into the lava!

"HELP!" screamed Larker.

Just then the **BOGEY MAN** stuck his
hand on to the girl's biscuit-tin helmet and
yanked her out of the way.

WHISK!

"NOOOO!" cried the **Giant Worm**. But it
was too late. The monster plunged into
the mouth of the volcano.

S I Z Z L E !

Yellow slime like thick custard oozed out of the **Giant Worm** as she was devoured by the lava.

SPLURGLE!

"You saved my life, **BOGEY MAN**," spluttered Larker.

"Well, it would have been rude not to," he replied.

"Did you know you can actually jump into a volcano? But only once!" she joked.

"I can't believe you're still cracking gags at a time like this!"

BOOF! BOOF! BOOF!

The **Giant Worm** was causing an explosive reaction within the volcano. Now the lava was blasting out of the pit.

"You're right!" replied Larker. "We need to get out of here! **And fast!**"

As quickly as he could, the **BOGEY MAN** whipped over to the exploded **MOnsterfication Machine** and rescued **Wormy.**

"A little singed," he said, inspecting his little friend. "But you will live. Now let's go!"

"The staircase is destroyed!" cried the **Giant Jelly**. "And it's all my stupid fault! It's impossible to get out!"

"Nothing's impossible!" exclaimed Larker. "There must be a way!"

"I have an idea. Everyone leap on my back!" suggested **Shark Boy**. "We can swim up to the invisible door."

And they did just that.

Unsteadily, **Shark Boy** took off and flew up to the top of the cave.

WHOOSH!

Now the molten lava was blasting skywards.

BOOF! BOOF! BOOF!

The volcano that the castle had been built on was erupting!

The heroes just managed to zoom out of the invisible door before the entire cave exploded.

KABOOM!

Chapter 54
VOLCANO

It was the middle of the night and the volcano was erupting under the castle. Every pupil had to get out alive.

So, as soon as they reached the ground level of the castle, Larker gave the order to the monsters.

"WE NEED TO FREE ALL THE KIDS! EVERY LAST ONE! TO THE BEDROOMS!"

Dino Girl smashed down the first door, setting the first child free.

BASH!

Not to be outdone, the **GIANT SLUG** did the same.

BOOM!

Then, of course, all the monsters wanted a go. In no time, they had smashed open every single door.

DOOF! KERUNCH! BAMM! THUNK!

When all the kids were gathered together, Larker called out to them: "Do not be alarmed by the monsters! I repeat:

DO NOT BE ALARMED BY THE MONSTERS!

It's a long story and we don't have time to go into it all right now because – and please don't panic – the school is about to be destroyed by a volcanic eruption!"

Well, if there is one thing to make people panic, it is to tell them NOT to panic and then tell them there is a volcanic eruption!

Immediately, panic erupted!

"STOP!" shouted Larker over the noise.

None of the kids listened.

"ROAR!" roared **Dino Girl.**

Suddenly, they all shut up.

"Thank you, **Dino Girl.** Everyone, this is really Daft!" The children all stared at the half human, half dinosaur in disbelief. "As I said, it's a long story. The only way out of the castle alive is to follow me! We need to go this way!"

With that, Larker held her arm up in the air and began marching down the hallway, away from the molten lava that was now oozing along the passage.

However, they'd only just turned the corner when they were confronted by the entire staff of **THE CRUEL SCHOOL.**

"Going somewhere, are we?" asked Meddle, who was at the front of the pack.

Behind him were Rank, Digits, Gibber, Dunk, the professor, Black, Ball, Bush and even the mysterious boatman.

"Yes, we are, actually. We're escaping from the volcanic eruption," declared Larker.

"No one escapes from **THE CRUEL SCHOOL!**" was the chilling reply.

"Oh, don't be a pain in the bum!" replied Larker. "Let us pass. You are all clockwork robots, anyway! Doktur Doctor called you her '**clockbots**'!"

"**Clockbots!**" they all cried in unison.

"No, we're not!" added Meddle.

"Yes, you are!" said Larker.

Meddle looked around to prompt his fellow staff members to join in, which they did.

"NO, WE'RE NOT!"

"Yes, you are!"

"NO, WE'RE NOT!"

"Yes, you are!"

"NO, WE'RE NOT!"

"Look, we don't have time for this!" said Larker.

"Toodle pip!" piped up the professor, her head, arms and legs all in the wrong sockets. **"Toodle pip! Toodle pip! Toodle pip!"**

"The headmistress is definitely a **clockbot!** Just look at her!" exclaimed Larker.

Meddle turned round and stared straight at the professor. "Yep, she might be a little bit **clockbotic** – I'll give you that! But she's the only one." Then he turned back to face Larker.

"You are all **clockbots!**" insisted Larker. "Trust me! Why do you think you all **tick?**"

"Do we?"

"YES!" chimed in all the monsters and kids.

Then behind the staff, Larker could see molten lava creeping along the hallway.

SIZZLE!

"Clockbots! Behind you!" shouted Larker.

"I'm not falling for that old one!" snorted Meddle.

"No, really. Behind you!"

"What do you think this is? An end-of-the-pier pantomime?"

Now the lava had reached the backs of the **clockbots**. No wonder they couldn't feel the intense heat, as they were made of metal.

"THIS WAY!" announced Larker. Her followers parted and she led them in another direction, away from the lava.

"Toodle pip!" repeated the professor. **"Toodle pip! Toodle pip! Toodle pip!"**

Meddle sighed with frustration. "Oh, do put a sock in it, Grandma!" he said, turning round.

Finally, the white-hot heat from the lava melted their wax skin.

Their metal skeletons were revealed.

"Me? A **clockbot?**" remarked Meddle, looking down at his metal arms and legs.

"Well, I never! NOW!

AFTER THEM!"

Chapter 55
METAL SKELETONS

Everywhere Larker led the kids and monsters through the castle, there was lava, lava and more lava. "We'll have to escape across the roof!" she exclaimed. One by one, she helped all the children out of the high window on to the roof, and then the monsters followed.

"Ladies first!" said the **BOGEY MAN.**

"No! No! No!" replied Larker. "Bogeys first!"

Her friend laughed and climbed out of the window.

Just as the girl climbed up too, she could feel someone or something grabbing hold of her leg.

"NOOO!" she cried.

Looking back inside the castle, she could see the metal skeleton of Meddle and all the other **clockbots** grabbing on to her leg. She even spied Digits's metal fingers.

Once again, that biscuit tin on her head came in useful. Larker pulled it off and began bashing all the metal hands away.

CLANK! CLINK! CLONK!

The lava now oozed all the way up to the ceiling. Just as she bashed the last metal hand away, the **clockbots** were demolished by the force of the lava.

"NOOOOOOOO!" cried the **clockbots** as they were imprisoned forever in the molten rock.

Larker ran across the roof of the castle, following the others. However, the white-hot lava below was melting the roof. With every leap she took, it collapsed behind her.

The poor pelican was still chained to one of the turrets.

"SQUAWK! SQUAWK! SQUAWK!"

went the bird in terror, feeling the intense heat of the lava beneath it.

Larker stopped to free it. She gave the pelican a kiss on the beak and threw it up in the air as she cried, "FLY! FLY FREE, POOR CHAINED-UP BIRD!"

The pelican did nothing of the sort. Instead, it crash-landed on the girl's head.

Now she wished she was still wearing that biscuit-tin helmet. The poor bird must have been out of flying practice.

Larker ran across the roof as it continued to collapse beneath her feet. Ahead, she could see the last of the monsters slide down a drainpipe on the side of the castle.

WHOOP!
WHOOP!
WHOOP!

"Hold on tightly!" said Larker to the pelican before they slid down the drainpipe.

WHOOP!

"Nice hat!" remarked the **BOGEY MAN.**

"Don't ask!" said Larker. "TO THE BOAT!"

The children and monsters surged forward. One by one, they slid down the rope ladder on the side of the cliff. Ahead was where the school's rowing boat was kept.

Just as Larker and the pelican grabbed hold of the ladder, the volcano exploded, taking the castle with it.

KABOOM!

They had all piled on to the boat and pushed themselves away from the rocks when the entire island crumbled into the sea.

GLOG! GLOG! GLOG!

In an instant, as if it had all been a bad dream, **THE CRUEL SCHOOL** was no more. The castle was now deep under the sea, never to be found again.

"WOW!" said Larker. "I can't believe it's gone."

"Gone forever!" added the **BOGEY MAN.**

"YES!"

shouted the children and monsters in

triumph.

Chapter 56
THE INKY BLACK SEA

The children rowed out to the inky black sea. All was still. All was quiet. Too still. Too quiet. Danger was not far away. Out of the deep, dark water, shapes began emerging.

SHARKS!

A shiver of sharks circled the rowing boat. At first, all you could see were the fins – before the jaws began snapping out of the water.

Just as the rowing boat was being thrown around in the waves, there was ANOTHER NASTY SURPRISE. Out of the box under the bench on the boat, a gnarled hand shot out and grabbed Larker's ankle.

"ARGH!" she screamed.

"**HURR!**" grunted Grunt as he slid out from his hiding place. As before, crouched atop his shiny dome was Fiend, the one-eyed, one-legged cat.

"**HISS!**" hissed Fiend, before sinking her teeth into Larker's other ankle.

"YIKES!" she yelped.

Grunt scrambled to his feet and began trying to push Larker off the boat as Fiend began swiping at the girl's face with her paw.

The cat's sharp claws were out, inches from Larker's nose.

"GIVE ME THAT OAR!" roared the **BOGEY MAN.**

His long, green, sticky arm reached across the boat and grabbed the last remaining oar from one of the children. He pulled it back, ready to strike.

"TAKE THIS, GRUNT!" shouted the **BOGEY MAN,** brandishing the long wooden weapon.

The force of the impact sent Grunt and his feline friend toppling into the water.

WHOOSH!

SPLOSH!
SPLOSH!

The **BOGEY MAN** reached out an oar.

"HERE! HOLD ON TO THIS!"

The cat leaped on to it and dragged herself with one paw up the oar.

Her master was not so lucky. Grunt went to grab the oar, but the biggest, hungriest shark dragged him down into the depths.

SNAP!

"*HURR!*" grunted Grunt for the final time.

There was quiet for a moment until the shark resurfaced and did a ginormous BURP.

"BURP!"

Then a metal skeleton shot out of the shark's mouth.

K E R C H A N G !

It flew through the air and landed in the water.

SPLOSH!

"Grunt was a **clockbot** too!" exclaimed the girl.

The once malevolent moggy curled up on the girl's lap and purred, as if she were the sweetest pet in the world.

"PURR!"

Larker looked down at it. Suddenly the cat looked adorable, and she couldn't help but stroke her. The pelican, however, had other ideas and did a poop in the cat's one good eye.

PLOP!

"HISS!"

Chapter 57
THE MONSTER GANG

Soon the welcoming lights of the coast were in sight.

"I told my horrible teacher Miss Clomp I would **escape**," said Larker. "I didn't know I would be taking everyone with me. Even the pelican!"

"And we all thought **escape** was impossible," replied the **BOGEY MAN.**

"Nothing's impossible!" said Larker with a grin.

"You have done a great thing, my friend! You set us all free!"

"We set ourselves free, remember?" she replied. "We did it – and could only have done it – together."

"SQUAWK!" agreed the pelican, still perched on her head.

"TOGETHER!" agreed all the children and monsters, now one happy band of friends.

Not long after that, they were all safely back on land.

The children hugged each other, so happy to be back in the world.

"Well, I suppose this is goodbye," said the **BOGEY MAN.**

"Does it have to be?" asked Larker, holding Fiend in her arms.

"What do you mean?"

"What if we remained a team of monsters? We could right wrongs for kids all over the world! We could call ourselves…

the Monster Gang!"

"I'm in!" said the **BOGEY MAN.**

"I would love to be part of the Monster Gang," added **Shark Boy**.

"Me too!" said **Dino Girl.**

"And me!" said the *Giant Jelly.*

"I'm there!" chirped **METEOR MAN.**

"Me as well!" said the **SLUG MONSTER.**

"Don't forget me!" said the **Atomic Amoeba.**

"Or me!" "Or ME!" "OR ME!" added all her multiples.

"MEOW!" meowed Fiend.

"SQUAWK!" added the pelican.

"EEK!" agreed a singed Wormy in the BOGEY MAN'S pocket.

"Then let's take to the skies!" exclaimed Larker.

"And find the very first mission for…

the Monster Gang!"

With that, they all took their places onboard Shark Boy and zoomed off high into the night sky.

It was time for a

whole new adventure.

THE END...?

If you enjoyed

MEGA
MONSTER

you are going to love
these other books by
David Walliams!

FING

Meet the Meeks!

Myrtle Meek has everything she could possibly want. But everything isn't enough. She wants more, more, MORE! When Myrtle declares she wants a FING, there's only one problem... What is a FING?

Mr and Mrs Meek will do anything to keep their darling daughter happy, even visit the spooky library vaults to delve into the dusty pages of the mysterious *Monsterpedia*. Their desperate quest leads to the depths of the jungliest jungle where the rarest creatures can be found. But will they ever find a FING?

SLIME

Welcome to
the Isle of Mulch...

This little island is home to a large
number of horrible grown-ups.

The school, the local park, the toy shop
and even the island's ice-cream van are all run
by awful adults who like nothing more than
making children miserable.

And the island is owned by the most awful
one of all – Aunt Greta Greed!

Something needs to be done about them.
But who could be brave enough?

Meet Ned – an extraordinary boy
with a special power: SLIMEPOWER!

ROBODOG

Welcome to the city of Bedlam.
Enter if you dare!

Bedlam is one of the most dangerous
places on Earth – home to a host of
wicked villains. Nothing and nobody
is safe from these evil criminals.

The city needs its own superhero
to defeat the super villains.

But who …? Robodog!

He's the newest recruit at the Police Dog
School, and supercharged for adventure.
But can he stop the most feared duo
in Bedlam, and their evil plans to
ruin the city …?